KILLER BLOW

DI SARA RAMSEY #2

M A COMLEY

JEAMEL PUBLISHING LIMITED

ACKNOWLEDGMENTS

Thank you as always to my rock, Jean, I'd be lost without you in my life.

Special thanks to Studioenp for creating such a superb cover.

My heartfelt thanks go to my wonderful editor Emmy Ellis @ Studioenp and to my fabulous proofreader Joseph Calleja for spotting all the lingering nits and my beta readers Jacqueline and Barbara.

Thank you also to Angela Guppy for allowing me to use her name in this book.

And finally, thank you to all the members of my wonderful ARC group for coming on this special journey with me and helping me to grow as an author. Love you all.

ALSO BY M A COMLEY

Blind Justice (Novella)

Cruel Justice (Book #1)

Mortal Justice (Novella)

Impeding Justice (Book #2)

Final Justice (Book #3)

Foul Justice (Book #4)

Guaranteed Justice (Book #5)

Ultimate Justice (Book #6)

Virtual Justice (Book #7)

Hostile Justice (Book #8)

Tortured Justice (Book #9)

Rough Justice (Book #10)

Dubious Justice (Book #11)

Calculated Justice (Book #12)

Twisted Justice (Book #13)

Justice at Christmas (Short Story)

Prime Justice (Book #14)

Heroic Justice (Book #15)

Shameful Justice (Book #16)

Immoral Justice (Book #17)

Toxic Justice (Book #18)

Unfair Justice (a 10,000 word short story)

Irrational Justice (a 10,000 word short story)

Seeking Justice (a 15,000 word novella)

Clever Deception (co-written by Linda S Prather)

Tragic Deception (co-written by Linda S Prather)

Sinful Deception (co-written by Linda S Prather)

No Right To Kill (DI Sara Ramsey Book 1)

Killer Blow (DI Sara Ramsey Book 2)

The Dead Can't Speak (DI Sara Ramsey Book 3)

Forever Watching You (DI Miranda Carr thriller)

Wrong Place (DI Sally Parker thriller #1)

No Hiding Place (DI Sally Parker thriller #2)

Cold Case (DI Sally Parker thriller#3)

Deadly Encounter (DI Sally Parker thriller #4)

Lost Innocence (DI Sally Parker thriller #5)

Web of Deceit (DI Sally Parker Novella with Tara Lyons)

The Missing Children (DI Kayli Bright #1)

Killer On The Run (DI Kayli Bright #2)

Hidden Agenda (DI Kayli Bright #3)

Murderous Betrayal (Kayli Bright #4)

Dying Breath (Kayli Bright #5)

The Hostage Takers (DI Kayli Bright Novella)

The Caller (co-written with Tara Lyons)

Evil In Disguise – a novel based on True events

Deadly Act (Hero series novella)

Torn Apart (Hero series #1)

End Result (Hero series #2)

In Plain Sight (Hero Series #3)

Double Jeopardy (Hero Series #4)

Sole Intention (Intention series #1)

Grave Intention (Intention series #2)

Devious Intention (Intention #3)

Merry Widow (A Lorne Simpkins short story)

It's A Dog's Life (A Lorne Simpkins short story)

A Time To Heal (A Sweet Romance)

A Time For Change (A Sweet Romance)

High Spirits

The Temptation series (Romantic Suspense/New Adult Novellas)

Past Temptation Lost Temptation

PROLOGUE

BERNICE WAVED at her daughter who was standing inside the dance studio awaiting her arrival. She rushed out of the car to meet her five-year-old daughter who ran into her arms. Bernice spun around—they'd had the same ritual for the past three months, since Bernice had signed Siobhan up for her modern dance class.

"Have you had a good time, sweetie?" Bernice knew she was asking a daft question; her daughter was beaming from ear to ear.

She lowered Siobhan to the ground. "The bestest, Mummy. How was your day?"

"Same as usual, always busy at work. Glad to be going home to be with you and Teddy. Grandma is picking him up from football practice, they should be home by now."

"Does that mean Grandma will be having dinner with us?"

Bernice opened the back door to the car and secured Siobhan with her seat belt. "Yes, we're having your favourite, spaghetti bolognese, tonight."

Siobhan hugged her round the neck and planted a sloppy kiss on her face. "You spoil us, Mummy. I love you soooooo much."

Bernice kissed her daughter's cheek and then the tip of her nose.

"You're worth spoiling. You two are the best kids a mother could wish to have. We're lucky to have each other, aren't we?"

"Yes, Mummy. Quick, let's get home. My tummy is beginning to hurt because I'm so hungwy."

Bernice left the door open and sought out her bag sitting on the passenger seat. Dipping into it, she pulled out a small golden delicious apple for her daughter. She handed it to an excited Siobhan and shut the back door. Once she was sitting behind the steering wheel, she pushed down the button to engage the central locking and set off. She had a twenty-minute journey ahead of her, and it was already beginning to get dark.

She couldn't wait to get home to her cute little cottage, to leave the bright lights of Hereford behind her for another day. They'd only moved out into the countryside around eighteen months ago, 'their own escape to the country' as she and her husband, Stuart, had called it. Hereford was getting busier and busier. The need to escape their hectic lifestyle had driven them out into the more rural parts of Herefordshire in search of their forever home. Their kids deserved to be brought up in a safe environment, where they could step outside their front door by themselves without the fear of anything bad happening to them.

Only last week, Bernice had gasped at the statistics on the news regarding child abductions in the area. Hence why she had taken to locking the car doors, even on the shortest of trips.

Bernice lowered the volume on the car stereo to have a conversation with Siobhan. She was a terrible chatterbox when the mood struck her.

"Mummy, we learnt some new tap steps today. It was fun."

"Ooo...you'll have to show us all this evening after we've had dinner."

"Cool. I love the new teacher. She showed me exactly what to do. I've been doing it wrong for weeks."

"That's wonderful, darling. I'm so pleased you're enjoying your lessons. What about being a dancer when you grow up, would you like that?" She looked at her daughter in the rearview mirror, and that was when she spotted the single headlight in the road behind.

Distracted, she missed Siobhan's reply. "Mummy? Are you listening to me?"

"Sorry, yes, sweetie. That's brilliant that you want to dance when you leave school."

"Mummy! You *didn't* listen to me."

Bernice cringed. She'd gambled she'd chosen the right option and failed. "I'm sorry, love, I must have misheard you. I thought you said you'd love to dance as a career."

"No. What I said was, I think I'd like to keep it as a hobby. I've decided I want to be a hairdresser. Is that all right?"

"If that's what you want to do, your father and I will support you in your decision. Have you given up on the idea of helping animals?"

"No. I'll do that in my spare time."

Bernice chuckled at the way her daughter appeared to have a handle on her young life and the dreams that lay ahead of her. Bernice's attention was drawn to the mirror again. The bike was getting closer—no, they'd dropped back a little. She rubbed at her eyes. Were they deceiving her in the dark?

No, the person behind kept up the momentum of speeding up and slowing down as though they were playing some sort of sadistic game with her.

Bernice pressed her foot down on the accelerator; they were only five minutes away from home now. The single headlight remained with her. She slowed down and so did the driver of the bike. She sped up, and the driver followed suit. Bernice had switched off from her daughter's wittering, intent on concentrating on the road ahead and the mirror, telling her what was going on behind her.

A bump jolted her. No, she must've imagined it. Siobhan fell silent. She glanced at the fear emanating from her daughter's eyes.

"Mummy, what was that?"

"Nothing, darling. I must have hit a stone in the road and it bounced up and hit under the car. Silly Mummy. Hard to avoid them in the dark."

Siobhan nodded, picked up her doll from the seat next to her and started talking to Jasmine.

Relief flowed through Bernice. The last thing she needed or wanted was an anxious child sitting behind her. However, that relief lasted only for an instant, until she felt another thud. *Back off, buster! Child on board, you moron.*

If this had been taking place during the day, she wouldn't have hesitated in pulling over and giving the driver a piece of her mind. There was no way she'd chance doing the same thing now, not when it was already pitch-black outside.

She stared at the bike rider in her mirror and eased her foot down on the accelerator again. When she glanced back at the road, something ran out in front of her. She yanked on the steering wheel to avoid hitting it. The car swerved viciously and surged into the trunk of a large tree on the edge of the road. The airbag deployed. Siobhan's petrified scream filled the car.

"It's all right, sweetie, silly Mummy had an accident. Are you okay?"

"No, Mummy, I'm scared. I need a cuddle, I think I hurt my wrist."

She held her little arm up in the air. Bernice winced. It looked broken. Her heart went out to Siobhan. She gasped, tears misting her vision.

Bernice reached over and laid a hand on her daughter's leg. "I need to ring for help, sweetheart. I know it hurts, but can you bear with me?" She scrabbled around in the dark, trying to locate her handbag. Finding it, she withdrew her phone and rang home. "Stuart, we've been in an accident. There was a man following us." She raised her head to look in the rearview mirror. The lone figure of a man filled the back window of the car. She let out a piercing scream.

"Bernice, Bernice, what's wrong?" Stuart said. "Oh my God, I'm coming. Where are you?"

"At the level crossing down the road, hurry. Please help us, Stuart." Panic and fear directed her next actions. She unlocked her car door and left the vehicle, her daughter's crying guiding her next movements as a mother's survival instinct kicked in. "What do you want from us? Leave us alone."

The man, dressed in black leathers and a large helmet with a lightning strike emblazoned on it, stiffened and walked slowly towards her. *Fight or flight, which is it to be?* Clenching her fists, she stood her ground. "Come on then, you mad fucker, let's see what you've got. I'm a black belt in karate." She took up the stance, ready for the imminent attack her instinct told her to expect.

The man faltered, then shrugged and upped his pace. The closer he got, the more Bernice's heart raced. If only she could keep him occupied until Stuart arrived to help her.

She shouted and chopped at the air with her hands, ensuring her attacker understood she meant business. She sensed his hesitation— or was that her imagination getting the better of her?

Suddenly, the man flew at her. One hard strike with his fist, and her legs crumpled beneath her. However, Bernice was back on her feet within seconds—she had a daughter to protect. He punched her again, flooring her. Bernice's jaw crunched, was it broken? Either way it wouldn't stop her from summoning up the energy she needed to protect her daughter until her husband showed up.

She bent her legs and struck the pose again. "Come on then! You won't keep me down."

"We'll see about that, woman."

He pounced, grabbed her arms with one of his and placed his other hand on the back of her head and smashed it against the car. Dazed, her legs gave way. She was drifting in and out of consciousness as concussion set in.

"No, please, not my daughter. Siobhan, run, go, sweetheart, run."

The man laughed and kicked her as he walked past. In the distance she thought she heard the car door open. Siobhan's scream became more intense. *Stuart, where are you?* She felt helpless, had no control over her limbs. She tried to stand, but her head lolled from side to side.

"Mummy, Mummy, help me..."

"I'm here, Siobhan, don't worry, Daddy is on his way." *Why? Why did I have to say that?*

The man rushed past her with her screaming daughter in his arms. Bernice's arms flailed as he swept past her. Damn, she'd misjudged her movements and failed to make contact with his legs. The darkness was closing in on her now. The bike started up. *No, please don't let him take her.* She fought the dizziness. An alarm went off in the distance. It took her a moment to figure out it was the level crossing barrier coming down. *God was finally on her side.* She pushed at the ground to sit up, her head still swaying as if a tonne weight was tied around her neck. She reached for the door handle on the car and eased herself to her feet.

The bike was at a standstill in front of the barrier. No sign of the train yet. She had time to get there. Her daughter was a mere ten feet ahead of her, she could make it, she had to.

"Mummy, Mummy, please, help me."

Siobhan lashed out at the man with her uninjured arm. He revved his engine, took a look over his shoulder and saw her approaching. Then he grabbed Siobhan around the waist, pulled her tight to him, angled his bike and dipped under the barrier.

"No. Please, come back. It's too dangerous."

They reached the other side, and the driver stopped as if goading her. Torment guiding her movements, she ducked under the barrier. When she straightened up again, her balance was shot. She staggered across the track, vibrations under her feet. Then came the sound of the train blasting its horn. She turned.

The lights blinded her before the train struck...

CHAPTER 1

"Hɪ, Jeff. What can I do for you?" DI Sara Ramsey was sitting at her desk, considering what to do about her evening meal when the desk sergeant rang her.

"I'm sorry, boss, I realise how late it is, but I thought you should know right away."

Her interest piqued, she sat upright in her chair. "Go on, Jeff, I can tell I'm not going to like it."

"You're not, boss." He sighed heavily. "The control room contacted me. They received a frantic emergency call from a man at a location. His wife has been struck by a train."

"Fuck. I mean, good heavens. Is she still alive?"

"Sadly not, but that's not all. The woman's husband arrived at the scene and has since reported his five-year-old daughter missing. She was with her mother at the time, you see."

Her heart racing, Sara shook her head. "All right, give me the location. I'll shoot over there now. In the meantime, I want you to issue an alert for the child, get it on the evening news if you can. You know how important the first twenty-four hours are in a case like this."

"I do. I'll get on it right away, boss."

"Thanks, Jeff." She slammed the phone down, tore her jacket off the back of the chair, fought her way into the arms, and then did the same with her coat while she ran into the incident room to address her team. "Heads-up, folks, we've got a dead woman killed by a train, also a possible missing child. Any thoughts of going home for the night have been put on hold for now. Make the necessary arrangements. Carla, we need to get over there, pronto."

Carla grabbed her jacket and followed her out of the incident room. "What about the child?" she asked, racing down the stairs behind Sara.

"It's all in hand; the usual procedures are in place."

"Do you think this is to do with the spate of child abductions we've had in the area recently?"

By now they had reached the car park and were running towards the car. "It's far too early to say. Let's hold fire on any judgement until we've been to the scene."

"Do you think this was an accident?" Carla asked, getting into the passenger seat beside her.

"Again, let's wait until we get there."

The ten-minute journey was conducted in silence apart from the odd sigh filling the car. When they arrived, there were two squad cars and a SOCO van, plus a motorbike that she recognised as belonging to the local pathologist, Lorraine Dixon. In the distance, one of the uniformed constables was comforting a distraught man. Sara presumed he was the husband.

"Hi, Lorraine, what have we got?"

Lorraine, who was crouched by the body, raised her head and asked, "You seriously don't want me to answer that, do you?"

Sara rolled her eyes. "You know what I mean."

"Fortunately, I do. The woman was struck by the train. My take is she ducked under the barrier. Could it be a suicide? I'm not sure, given the woman's daughter appears to be missing. Maybe she felt she'd failed the daughter and decided to end it all. Or perhaps she was trying to reach her daughter and out of sheer desperation crossed the track without considering the consequences."

Sara tutted. "Either way, the result is evident. Do you have anything I can give the husband? I take it that's him." She jabbed a finger over her shoulder.

"It is. He rang it in. He told me he was on his way to help her."

Sara looked up the road at what appeared to be the woman's car, smashed into a tree. "She had an accident? Could she have been dazed? That's why she stumbled into the path of the train?"

Lorraine nodded. "Possibly. I hope you've got an alert out for the kiddie."

"First thing I did. You don't need to check up that I'm doing my job right, my DCI sees to that."

Looking ashamed, Lorraine glanced down at the corpse, which was thankfully intact. Sara had been to many of these types of scenes before and witnessed the bodies of the victims sliced in two. Usually the investigation had led them to discover the victim had suicide tendencies. Sara wasn't getting that impression in this case.

"If the last view she had of her daughter was her being abducted, Lord knows what torment the woman was going through at the time of her death," Lorraine said.

"Exactly. Heartbreaking. I'm gonna have a word with the husband if you have nothing else for me."

"I haven't. I need to crack on. They want the railway track up and running ASAP. I'll make my initial assessment then get the body moved, either to the side of the road or back to the mortuary."

"Send your report through as soon as you can."

"I will."

Sara and Carla strode towards the man, who leaned against his car with a male constable blocking his view of his wife.

"Hello, sir. I'm DI Sara Ramsey, and this is my partner, DS Carla Jameson."

"Have you caught the bastard yet?"

"Sorry, not yet. We have a team working hard to get your daughter back. Mr Wisdom, can you tell me when your wife rang you and fill me in on the conversation you had with her?"

"She told me someone was following her and that she'd had an accident. I'll never forget her scream. I told her that I would come immediately. She hung up believing I was on the way. I need to find my daughter. She's only five."

"We'll do our best, sir. Do you have a recent photo?"

He withdrew his phone from his pocket and tapped in the password, then handed the phone to Sara. "That's Siobhan, she's five years old," he repeated as if to ram the notion home to them. "Please, you have to bring her back to me. With her mother d…now gone, Siobhan and Teddy are all I have left in this world."

"We'll do our best. Carla, can you take a photo on your phone for me?" She passed Carla the phone. "Mr Wisdom, can you tell me who you think might be behind this?"

His eyes bulged. "How should I know? That's your job to investigate. Isn't that how these things work? And it's Stuart."

"Stuart, you're right, of course it's our job, but we also need some guidance from you as to where to start our enquiries. Have either you or your wife had any cause for concern lately? Someone making threats, perhaps? Have you spotted a stranger lingering outside your house? Did your wife tell you if there had been a stranger seen at her place of work or outside the school? Anything along those lines?"

"No. Nothing. This is all news to me. When she rang, she said someone was following her."

"Okay, that's a start. We'll regard this as a random attack from now on. Where is your son, Stuart?"

"At home with his grandmother, Bernice's mum, Katherine. Bloody hell, how am I going to break the news to her that her daughter is de…?"

"Is she back at your house?"

"Yes, we were due to have a family dinner. Katherine picked Teddy up from football. Bernice was fetching Siobhan from her dance class. I can't believe this is happening." Tears dripped onto his cheeks. "That this is the last time I will ever see my wife. She didn't deserve to die, not now, not like this." His hands covered his face, and a sob erupted.

Sara swallowed down the knot of emotion in her throat, aware only too well of how great the grief could be when a spouse died. She stared at the man, not really knowing how to comfort him without breaking down herself.

Thankfully, Carla took over. "Mr Wisdom, why don't we take you home? You'll be better off there. Let the pathologist and her team do what's necessary here."

He stared blankly at Carla. Sara gave herself a good talking to and nodded at Carla, letting her know she was okay. Together, the three of them walked back to Sara's car.

"We'll leave your car here. I'll arrange for someone to drop it off at the house, if you like?"

"I'll pick it up tomorrow." He pointed the key fob at the vehicle to lock it, then opened the back door and slipped into Sara's car.

The only words he spoke during the journey were to give them directions. When Sara parked outside his home, a woman in her sixties peered out of a window on the ground floor.

"How the hell am I going to tell her?" he muttered.

Sara sighed. He must have been too traumatised when he'd found his wife to ring his mother-in-law. *Damn, this is going to be tough.* "Would you rather tell her alone?"

He shook his head. "No. I think it will help if you're there. I know that makes me sound like a coward, but Bernice was her daughter, her only daughter, her only child. Oh heck, how am I going to tell her that she's de…?"

Sara turned in her seat to look at him. "I'll go in there and do it for you. You have your own grief to contend with. No one is expecting you to set that aside."

His gaze rose to meet hers. "Maybe I should do this alone. Just give me a second to collect my thoughts."

"Take all the time you need."

Moments later, he yanked on the handle to open the back door and stepped out. "Will you give me a few minutes?"

"Sure. Just signal for us to come in when you need us."

With his shoulders slouched, he made his way up the narrow path. The woman left the window and rushed to open the front door. She glanced over Stuart's shoulder at Sara and Carla still sitting in the car.

Stuart managed to get her inside and closed the door. There was silence in the car until the woman's scream filtered the air.

"Fuck! Why does life have to be so cruel?" Sara's head hit the steering wheel as her own depressing memories stirred.

Carla sighed. "Are you going to be able to cope in there? I'm not being funny, but given what you've been through in the past, I saw how it affected you back there."

"I'll be fine. Come on, let's get this over with. The sooner we get the answers we need, the sooner we can leave these good people to grieve."

"Do you think they'll be able to do that? I mean, with the kid still missing..." Carla replied.

Sara lashed out at the steering wheel. For a moment, that particular dilemma had slipped her mind. "We need to get back to the station. I know we usually support the families at times like this, but we're wasting time."

"You need to tell them that. I'm sure they'll understand."

Sara got out of the car. "Do you want to wait here? No point in both of us dealing with this shit."

"If you think that's the right way to go about things. Want me to check in with the rest of the team?"

"Yep. Get them searching the CCTV footage in this area. There must be cameras around the track. Let's see what we can glean from that and go from there."

"Will do."

Sara slammed her car door shut and walked towards the house. She swallowed down the bile rising in her throat when the woman sobbed on the other side of the door. She knocked gently.

Stuart opened the door, his arms wrapped around his mother-in-law. "Come in. Katherine, this is the inspector in charge of the case."

Sara smiled and nodded at the woman. "I'm so sorry for your loss."

Katherine pulled away from her son-in-law and wiped her nose on a hanky she extracted from her sleeve. "Come in. What are you going to do about this? Do you know who is responsible?"

Sara glanced past the two adults in the hallway when she heard a child crying on the stairs. "Stuart, you might want to see to your son."

It was as if the man hadn't realised the child was there. "Oh God," he mumbled then raced up the stairs to pick up his son. He took the child into one of the bedrooms.

"Katherine, shall we go somewhere where we can chat?"

"Come through to the kitchen. Do you want a drink?"

"Not for me. You have one, though." Sara followed the woman through the brightly decorated hallway into the vast kitchen at the rear. The room felt homely, and the smell emanating from the stove made Sara feel hungry.

Katherine switched off the gas under the pot and filled the kettle. Seemingly on autopilot, she dropped teabags in a couple of mugs and added the sugar and milk.

"All right if I sit down?" Sara asked.

Katherine looked dazed. "I'm sorry, go right ahead." She joined Sara at the table. "Why? Why has this happened? Bernice has never hurt anyone in her life. Even at school she was the most popular girl. Everyone liked her, so why would someone target her, target *us*, like this?"

"We've yet to discover that. We will, though, I assure you. Has Bernice mentioned lately if something didn't fit right with her? By that I mean, has she said anything about someone maybe following her, something like that?"

Katherine stared down at her mug which she was gripping in both hands. "No, nothing as far as I know. We're simple people, lead very simple lives. There's no need for anyone to feel envious of what we have. Unless..."

Sara's interest surged. "Unless?"

"Is this about Siobhan?"

Sara tutted. "We're not sure yet. We're aware of several child abductions taking place over the past month or so."

"I heard about it on the news. Have you found any of the children yet?"

"Sadly not."

13

"That's not exactly reassuring."

"I know. I'm sorry. We're working alongside several other teams to ensure the children are found quickly."

"What do you think will happen to them if you don't find them?" She held up her hand. "No, don't tell me. I couldn't handle the truth." She buried her head in her hands and sobbed again, repeating the word 'why' over and over.

Stuart walked into the room. He immediately rushed over to Katherine and knelt beside her. "Katherine, I know how hard this is, but please, we must remain strong. The kids will need us to be that over the coming few days."

Sara smiled and nodded as he glanced her way for reassurance. "Stuart, is there anything you can tell me that might give us some clue as to what is going on here? Can you recall falling out with anyone, either you or Bernice, in the last few months?"

"No, absolutely not. My wife and I are gentle people. We're family-oriented and devote all our time to our kids, rarely mix with people other than our family, except at a few social gatherings connected to the local school."

"I see. May I ask what you do for a living?"

"I own a local canning factory with my partner, Grayson Lee."

"How long has your business been up and running?"

"Five years, just over, I suppose."

"Have you had any problems, possibly from rival firms owning the same kind of business?"

He shook his head. "There really isn't anyone else in our line of business around here. What? You think this has to do with *me*?"

Sara shrugged. "It's possible. Let's say it's not unheard of in cases such as this."

"That's incredible. To think people would use someone else's children as pawns in a dangerous game like this."

"I'm not saying that's what has happened, but it's a possible route we have to go down. In all probability, this was just a random attack on your wife and daughter."

"Either scenario is sickening that leaves my wife dead and my child abducted. How am I going to cope without them?" Stuart sank into the chair next to his mother-in-law.

Katherine reached out and placed a hand over his. "With my help. We'll get through this, Stuart. I promise you we will, if only for Teddy's sake."

He sniffled and wiped his nose on the sleeve of his jumper. "He asked me what had happened. I couldn't tell him, I struggled to form the words. It's too unbearable to think they're both gone, and in Siobhan's case gone, possibly, never to return."

"We don't know that yet, Mr Wisdom. Please don't give up hope now, our investigation is only just beginning. I can promise you we'll do everything in our power to bring your daughter back to you."

"I hope so, Inspector, because she's all I've got, apart from Teddy, of course."

"I'll give you one of my cards. If anything comes to mind after I've gone that you think I should know about, please ring me."

Katherine took the card and nodded. "We will. We'll try and think of someone. From my point of view, I can't imagine anyone linked to either Stuart or Bernice...who would dream of doing this." Her voice caught as she mentioned her daughter's name.

"You stay there. I can see myself out. Hopefully, I'll be in touch with some good news for you soon. Rest assured that my team and I will work hard to achieve a positive outcome."

"Thank you, Inspector," Stuart replied, his eyes brimming with fresh tears.

Sara left the house and climbed into the driver's seat of her car and placed her head on the steering wheel.

"Everything all right?" Carla asked, concerned.

"Apart from a little girl being abducted from what appears to be a genuinely nice family, yes, everything is just dandy." She leant back and faced Carla. "Sorry, you didn't deserve that sarcastic retort."

"It's fine. I've learnt to expect it from you." Carla chuckled, clearly trying to break through the icy atmosphere.

"Gee, thanks. Any news from the team?"

"Nothing yet. They had already requested the CCTV footage. Two of them are in the process of viewing it now. What's our next step?"

"Go back to the station. Are you all right with working late tonight?"

"I am. Andrew is away on a course anyway, so my time is my own."

"Good. I'd like to stick with this. Hopefully something will come to light overnight, a clue that will lead us to little Siobhan."

"Fingers crossed on that one. The poor mite must be out of her mind with fear. I hope we find her soon before…well, I don't have to fill in the gap for you on that one, do I?"

"Nope. I have a pretty vivid imagination, too vivid at times in cases such as this." Sara started the engine and pulled away from the kerb. "The main question we need to be asking is whether the child abductions in this area are linked to this case."

"My take at this early stage is, I'm just not sure. It's different. In each of the other cases, no one else was hurt or killed."

Sara chewed the inside of her mouth and then said, "You might have something there. We'll need to get in touch with the missing persons team all the same, marry things up and go from there."

When they arrived back at the station, Sara was proud of what her team had accomplished so far. She'd been with them a little over a year since arriving from Liverpool; however, with each passing case, she got to like them more and more.

Barry Thomas, a constable who'd transferred from Pontypool around the same time as Sara, was busy searching through the CCTV footage along with Craig Watson, the youngest and most enthusiastic member of the team. Sara stopped by Barry's desk while Carla carried on to the vending machine to buy them both a coffee.

"Anything we can use yet, Barry?" Sara perched on the desk next to his and leant forward, pressing her hands down on her thighs.

"We located the moped that appeared to be used to harass the deceased. We're searching the other footage in the area trying to piece together what actually happened." He selected an image and ran the disc.

Sara looked at the monitor through narrowed eyes. "So the bike was following her and started bumping her vehicle up the backside, is that what I'm seeing?"

"It would appear that way. Although, I can't see that she did anything wrong to trigger any anger from the moped driver."

"From that I take it you're saying that she was intentionally targeted?"

"It seems that way to me, boss."

Carla joined the group and handed Sara a cup of coffee. She leant in as Barry replayed the footage. "Whoa! She must have been terrified. Do we know how long he was tailing her for?"

"My guess at this point, although I have to corroborate it, would be around ten minutes," Barry replied.

"Ten minutes of sheer terror before her life ended," Sara shook her head in disgust. "Do we know how the accident occurred?"

Barry ran the disc again, picking up from where the moped bumped Bernice's car up the backside. They watched as Bernice appeared to put her foot down only to slam on the brakes moments later and swerve across the road into a large tree.

"She tried to avoid something in the road. Was that a cat or a dog? Never mind, it doesn't really matter."

"I think it was a cat. Hard to tell really," Barry said.

"Okay, does the footage show how they got out of the car? If I were Bernice, I think I would have felt safer in the vehicle than on foot. What about you guys?"

The three of them nodded, then Carla added, "Maybe she received a bump to the head during the impact that made her react irrationally."

"Maybe. Can you wind it forward a bit, Barry? Also, can you make out a registration number on the bike?"

"Nope, it was covered in mud; I zoomed in for a closer look earlier. I'm going to show a couple of different angles now." He pressed a button on his keyboard, and the image sped up on the monitor. He paused it a few seconds later once the car collided with the tree, then hit another button to bring up an image from another camera.

Sara watched the events unfold with bated breath. Bernice got out of the vehicle and shouted at the driver of the moped. He dismounted his bike and walked towards her. Bernice retreated a little, her bravery fading. He punched her a couple of times. She struck the pose of a karate expert before the driver then slammed Bernice's head onto the roof of the car.

Sara winced. "Ouch. Well, if she wasn't concussed before, she damn well would've been after that blow. She tried her hardest to challenge him, but her signs of bravery only seemed to aggravate the driver further."

"Why? Why did the driver do that? Because she mouthed off at him?" Carla asked.

Sara sighed and blew out a long breath. "Who knows? All the poor woman was doing was protecting her child. At least that's what it looks like to me."

"Me, too," Barry said. "There's more."

They saw the moped driver walk around the side of the car and open the back door. He emerged a few seconds later with Bernice's daughter in his arms. Sara's eyes filled up with tears. The child was distressed, reaching out and crying for her mother who was lying on the ground next to the car.

The man did nothing to help Bernice. Instead, he strode past her and mounted the bike again. He yanked the child into place in front of him and approached the level crossing just as the alarm went off and the barrier dropped in front of him. The driver glanced over his shoulder several times. At the edge of the camera, Sara spotted Bernice getting to her feet. Wandering in a dazed state, she approached the crossing. This must have spooked the driver because he tipped the bike sideways and went under the barrier. Bernice waved her arms, obviously crying out for her daughter. The bike stopped on the other side of the track. "Is he taunting her?"

"Seems more like goading her to me," Carla stated, her gaze glued to the screen.

"I'm not sure I can see the rest," Sara admitted, aware of what happened next.

"Want me to stop it?" Barry asked.

Sara inhaled a large breath and shook her head. "No, you might as well carry on."

The next image showed Bernice ducking under the barrier and stumbling onto the track. Suddenly she was bathed in a bright light. Sara squeezed her eyes shut. Several gasps broke out around her as the train made contact with the victim.

"All right, turn it off, Barry."

Barry tapped his keyboard.

Sara opened her eyes and scanned the team. "I don't know about you guys, but I feel sick. Whether this guy's actions were intentional or not, I'm guessing that he'd known how Bernice would react when he abducted her child; therefore, we can throw the book at him when we finally catch up with him."

"If we catch up with him," Carla suggested.

"We have to pull out all the stops on this one, team. I'll get in touch with missing persons first thing in the morning. We'll need to look into all the ongoing cases of child abduction in the area in the past few months. My gut is telling me these cases are linked. Don't ask me why. God, I hope we can find these kids."

"The incident was being aired on the local news this evening. Maybe someone who knows something will come forward. Here's hoping anyway," Carla replied, her voice trailing off.

Distracted, Sara nodded. "Barry, go over the footage again, right back to the beginning. Actually, before that even. Oh gosh, I'm not making any sense, my mind is working faster than my mouth can keep up. Let me start again. I want you to see if you can pinpoint where the moped began following Bernice. Try and locate any footage from the city. There must have been something that triggered his interest in Bernice's car in the first place. I think if we can find out what that is it'll help solve the case, or at least figure out who the culprit is. Of course, I could be talking a load of bollocks, but let's try."

"No, I think you might have something, boss. I'll get on it right away."

Sara smiled her appreciation. "I hate to ask, but is everyone okay to work late?"

The team either responded verbally or nodded.

"Great, you're all brilliant. I'm going to put in an order for pizza in that case. Anyone fancy anything specific?"

"I'll eat anything with the exception of pineapple," Craig replied.

"What is it with you men and pineapple? I love a slice of ham and pineapple myself."

Craig placed two fingers in his mouth, imitating he wanted to make himself sick.

Sara shook her head and pulled a face at him. "So, tell me what you want instead? I haven't got time to clear up anyone's vomit this evening."

The team chuckled and then placed their order. Sara jotted down their requests and went into her office to make the call. The person at the pizza parlour told her it was their busiest time and the order could take up to an hour before being delivered.

Sara popped her head around the office door to relay the unhappy message to the team and then sat behind her desk. Something was niggling her about the moped rider, and she struggled to put her finger on what that something was. Sitting in her chair, she closed her eyes and ran through the footage again in her mind. After she'd finished, she picked up the phone and dialled Stuart Wisdom.

"Hello, Mr Wisdom, this is DI Sara Ramsey. I'm sorry to ring so late."

"It's fine. I'm just sitting here thinking. Have you got some news for me?"

"Sorry, no. What I wanted to know was if you knew anyone who rode a moped."

"What type of question is that?" he responded with a question of his own.

"I know it sounds a little odd. Do you?"

A momentary silence filled the line. "No, I can't think of anyone."

"What about colleagues, neighbours possibly?"

"No. No one I can think of, why?"

She exhaled a breath. "We've been looking over the CCTV footage of the accident. It would appear your wife was being followed by someone on a moped who caused her to crash."

"When she rang me, she told me she was being followed, I just presumed she meant by someone in a car. This person took Siobhan, too, right? Or did someone else do that?"

"No, it was the same person."

"Why? I want my daughter back, Inspector. If she saw what happened to Bernice, she's going to be frantic, let alone traumatised. Scared shitless even."

"I know. I promise you, we're doing everything we can to find her, hence my call about the moped."

"No, I don't know anyone. Please find her soon. I'm going out of my mind with worry here. Ring me day or night if there's anything else you want to know. I doubt I'll be able to sleep much knowing that my daughter is in the hands of a madman." His voice caught in his throat and he broke down.

Sara swallowed the emotion tearing her apart. "Please, Stuart, try and hang in there, if only for your son's sake."

"I'm trying. It's so hard, though. Do you have children, Inspector?"

"No. That doesn't mean that I don't understand what you're going through. My team and I are doing our best to get Siobhan back to you, I promise."

His shuddering breath filled the line between them. "Okay, I don't have any other option but to believe you. Please, keep me informed of your progress."

"You can be assured of that, sir. Try and rest. You might want to avoid the news this evening. There will be an appeal going out on all stations."

"Glad to hear it. Hopefully something good will come of it."

"We're hoping that will be the case, too, sir. I'll be in touch soon."

"Thank you for ringing."

Sara hung up and wiped away the tears that were threatening to fall from her eyes. To occupy her mind, she turned her attention to the mounting paperwork on her desk until Carla knocked on her door thirty minutes later to let her know the pizza had arrived. As soon as the smell wafted into her office, her tummy rumbled. They all needed sustenance for the long evening ahead of them. Leaving her office, Sara made a beeline for the vending machine where she bought the whole team a drink before settling down to the much-anticipated pizza.

Carla switched on the TV when she saw Sara's gaze drift over to the screen. Sara smiled at her partner who was beginning to understand her more and more each day since she'd begun opening up to her about what had gone on in her past.

The newscaster announced a roundup of all the main headlines. Sara was saddened to see that Siobhan's disappearance wasn't being treated as urgent. She grabbed the remote control and turned over to *Sky News*. At least they were running a strapline at the bottom of the screen mentioning the little girl, along with the death of her mother and a hotline number that would direct any likely calls coming in to the incident room.

"I hope the phones light up soon," Carla mumbled.

"Me, too. I don't know where to turn if they don't. Barry, I know it hasn't been long and what you've come up with so far has been superb, but have you managed to trace the moped after it left the level crossing?"

"That's a negative, boss. The cameras don't stretch out into the sticks, and those at the level crossing were the last on that road."

She slammed a fist into her thigh and tore off another slice of pizza from the box on the desk beside her. "We need to catch a break soon, guys. I fear what might happen to the child if we don't. Thanks again for staying on tonight. I hope it doesn't turn out to be a waste of time."

"It's not a waste of time to me if there's free pizza involved, boss," Craig said, flashing a greasy grin.

Sara bit off the crust from her slice of pizza and threw it at him. She missed by six inches or so. "Damn, my aim isn't getting any better."

"Thankfully." Craig chuckled.

The ringing phone put a halt to their banter.

Sara finished chewing her mouthful of pizza and answered the call herself. "DI Sara Ramsey, you're through to the incident room, how may I help?"

"Umm…I'm not sure if this has anything to do with the case that's all over the news tonight, but I thought I'd ring up and check anyway."

Sara clicked her fingers, instructing a team member to lower the volume on the TV. "Can you start by giving me your name, sir?"

"Jaden Pratt. I know, I've heard all the jokes under the sun."

"My lips are sealed regarding that, sir. Okay, what can you tell me?"

"I was driving home from work this evening when I passed a moped. The driver was all kitted up in the right gear, but his passenger, a small child, had no protective headwear or clothing on. I thought it was strange at the time. I blasted my horn at the driver and gestured for him to pull over for a chat, but he gave me the finger and floored the bike."

"Ouch, can you tell me where you were at the time, sir?"

"In Greenock Road, close to the level crossing, heading east of the city. I know, thinking about it now, I really should have put in a call to the police at the time. I just thought it was someone taking their kid on a spin around the neighbourhood as a prank. Never dreamt anything like what I've seen reported on the news would come of it."

"Did you see which direction the bike was heading in, sir?"

"It took off in one direction but a few minutes later it passed me going back into the city. It's anyone's guess, I suppose. Christ, if it's the same person who abducted the child, I'm going to be kicking myself for not getting involved for years to come."

"Please don't beat yourself up about it, sir. You've done the right thing by informing us now. It's given us more than we had before. Hopefully, someone else will ring up as you have and add to what you've already told us. That's often how these things work. So no recriminations, okay?"

"If you say so. I take it the child is still missing then?"

"She is at present. Would you mind if I sent a uniformed officer around to take a statement, sir?"

"Not at all. Tonight?"

"Preferably. Is that okay?"

"Fine. My address is forty-three Winchester Avenue."

"Expect someone out to you within the next few hours."

"I will do. I hope you find the child."

"So do we, sir. Thank you for contacting us." Sara ended the call and addressed the team. "Apparently, the caller tried to flag the moped driver down out of concern for the child, but all that accomplished was to make the driver put his foot down. Moments later he saw the moped drive past him and head back into the city. It's going to be like finding the proverbial needle. I'm not hopeful his call will lead to anything."

"It's more than we had ten minutes ago," Carla replied.

Barry turned his chair back to his desk and threw his slice of pizza in the box. "I'll keep searching the CCTV. Maybe I'll locate the bastard in another area of the city."

"Good luck with that one. You have a vast area to cover, Barry."

"Correction, boss, *we* have a vast area to cover. Craig, stop stuffing your face and get cracking on another monitor."

Craig leapt out of his chair and rushed to the desk closest to Barry. The rest of the team took their departure from the seating area as the green light to get back to work. Christine Miller and Carla took it upon themselves to man the phones while Jill Smalling and Will Rogerson began the background checks on the family and Mr Wisdom's business and partner.

The phones rang continuously until the witching hour; however, Sara was disappointed by the lack of leads from the other phone calls. Only Jaden Pratt's information stood out, but then that really hadn't amounted to much in their favour.

Feeling desperately tired at just gone one, Sara decided to send the team home. Some of them whined, saying that they had a good few hours left in them, but others nodded in agreement.

"I appreciate some of you wanting to continue, but it's getting late.

There's little more we can do now. Let's pack up and start afresh in the morning."

She dipped into the office to fetch her coat and switched off the light. The rest of the team followed her out of the incident room and down the stairs to the car park.

She bid them all farewell. "See you at nine, not a moment sooner in the morning, got that?"

Carla raised an eyebrow and tilted her head. "And is that what time you'll show up in the morning?"

Sara grinned. "I might do. There really is no fooling you, is there? Don't come in early. You and the rest of the team deserve a bit of a lie-in."

"If you're coming in early then so am I. You know what I'm like when Andrew is away."

"I know. Look, it's entirely up to you. Don't feel obliged to do it, though."

"I never feel obliged when it gets me out of tidying up at home. Nothing worse than suffering through doing a bit of housework when there's an urgent case to solve. And forgive me if I'm wrong, but this case is urgent, right?"

Sara narrowed her eyes. "You know damn well it is. Go on, get out of here. I'm never going to win this particular argument, am I?"

"You're not, no." Carla waved and dropped into the driver's seat of her vehicle.

Sara waved and did the same.

Twenty minutes later, she pulled onto her drive. The new estate Sara lived on, which was due to be completed within the next few months, was deathly quiet. She softly closed her car door and let herself into the house. Misty, her tortoiseshell cat, was there to greet her like always. She bent down to take her shoes off and swept the cat into her arms. "Hello, sweetie. Have you missed me?" Misty rubbed her head against her cheek and under her chin. "I take it that was a yes. You must be hungry. Let's see what we can find you in the cupboard."

Placing the cat on the floor, she stepped into the kitchen and switched on the light. She groaned when yesterday's washing up stared back at her from the sink. "I knew I'd regret not doing that this morning before leaving." She ran the hot water and dashed across the kitchen to the pantry cupboard where she kept Misty's dry food along with the tins, then she rushed back to switch off the water and cursed the fact there was no hot water. "Damn, I forgot to put the boiler on again. When will I bloody learn?" She reached across the worktop and hit the booster button on the heating control. It lit up, and the boiler kicked in right away.

Sara smiled when Misty began a figure of eight around her legs, anxious for her food to be put down. "All right, it's coming, I promise. Be patient, munchkin." She opened the tin and placed half of it in the cat's bowl and added a sprinkling of dried food over the top. "You have to eat it. Vet Mark says it's good for your teeth. Mentioning Mark's name made her tummy flutter. If it had been several hours earlier in the evening, she would have rung him for a chat. There was no way he'd welcome a call disturbing his sleep at this hour of the morning. No, she'd put that notion on hold for now.

They had been on several dates over the past few months. The last thing she wanted to do was give him the impression she was falling for him, because although her knees went a little weak when she laid eyes on him, there were still a certain amount of awkward moments during the course of their dates that led her to have serious doubts as to whether they had a future together. Now and again, she had to push aside the little devil voice telling her to dump him. She wondered if other widows, who had been deeply in love with their husbands before their death, ever felt the same way she did. How many good relationships crashed and burned when a niggling doubt set in?

Mark had never said, or indeed done, anything to upset her. Any reservations she had about her relationship were totally her fault. At the end of the day, there was nothing she could do about setting her fears aside. Was it fear? Or was she foolishly misreading the signs? What exactly was going on in her head? Was it a matter of having trust issues? No, she didn't think so. Maybe it was more to do with her feeling guilty. Guilty because she was trying to move on with her life. Maybe deep down she wasn't ready to do that. Perhaps that explained the awkward moments on their dates.

"I'm an utter idiot. I have the chance of finding happiness again, the type of opportunity that only happens once in a blue moon, and up goes the damn wall. Why? Mark is a genuinely nice guy. He's kind to animals—that's always a telling sign if someone has a compassionate side or not. Mum would tell me I'm being a fool to have all these doubts, not that Mark has tried to take things further. There will never be another Philip, but Mark has to be the next best thing, doesn't he?"

After letting Misty out and making sure she ate all her food, she made herself a cup of hot milky chocolate and went to bed. Sitting up in bed, her thoughts focused on the child who was missing, and she made a silent vow to bring the innocent victim home, unharmed. Then she settled down, turned off the bedside light and snuggled up with Misty. Sleep evaded her, though. She reached for her phone in the dark and pressed the familiar button that would lead to Philip's last voicemail message to her. She found the words a great source of comfort, even though they were the final words she'd ever hear him say.

"Hello, darling. I'm running late. I'll be with you in five. Love you to the moon and back."

Sara returned the phone to the bedside table and smiled, at peace with the fact she'd felt Philip around her since his death. Not in a hair-raisingly spooky way. No, in a way that said a lot about the man he was—a caring, comforting way. She missed not being able to cuddle up to him at night. Misty would have to suffice for now, until something better came along.

See, Mark must be getting under my skin. There's no way I would have had those types of thoughts six months ago.

She drifted off to sleep soon after and dreamt about both men.

CHAPTER 2

SARA WAS SITTING behind her desk at eight-thirty the next morning, coffee in hand and wading through a mound of brown envelopes when Carla poked her head around the door.

"I knew you'd get in early," her partner said, pointing a finger.

"Ditto. You look rough. Dare I ask if you got any sleep?"

"Not much. The little one was on my mind all night. What about you?"

"I slept eventually. Although I can't lie, Siobhan was on my mind, too, amongst other things." She bit down on her tongue as soon as the words escaped.

Carla's eyes widened, and she tilted her head. "Are you going to tell me what you meant by that?"

"Another time perhaps. We have work to do. Let me know when the rest of the team get here. Until then, I'll be immersed in this lot."

Carla tutted, aware she was being dismissed, and left the room. "Do you want another coffee?" she called out.

"I never say no to a top-up, thanks, Carla."

Moments later, Carla brought her drink and placed it on the desk. "Everyone is here, so we're ready when you are."

"Thanks, I'll be right out." Once Carla had left the room, Sara smiled to herself, pleased her team were apparently taking this case seriously enough to show up early. She was proud of them.

She downed the dregs of her old coffee, picked up her fresh drink and wandered into the incident room. "Morning, all. I really appreciate you coming in early, even though we all had a late night. Let's hope that decision goes in our favour. I want to hit the ground running today. Carla and I will be working with the missing persons department—maybe we'll find a link there that we can work with. I want the rest of you to continue what you were doing yesterday regarding the background checks on the family and their known associates, plus the CCTV footage. Let's broaden the search on that, Barry. Let me know if you spot the bastard. Maybe you'll locate the bike when it has a clean number plate we can work on. I'll live in hope on that one. Craig, can you search the database for me? I want you to specifically focus on other moped-related crimes in the past six months."

"Will do, boss. Would that be just in the Hereford area or do you want me to extend the search?"

"Let's extend that to a fifty-mile radius, that should cover it."

The young constable nodded.

Sara clapped, drawing the meeting to a close. "Good, good. Hit it hard and fast, guys, we've got a precious child relying on us to save her. Carla, are you ready?"

Her partner left her seat and followed her out of the room and up one flight of stairs to the missing persons department. They found Maddy Powell slipping her jacket on the back of her chair. She smiled when they entered the room.

"Hello, you two. What can I do for you on this crisp February morning?" Maddy was the perfect person for the role, always bright and breezy, keen to reunite people with their loved ones. She'd had huge success in the area over the years, too.

"Hi, Maddy, it's not too early to seek your expertise, is it?" Sara asked, pulling out a chair and sitting.

"Not at all. Sounds serious. Wait a minute, has this got something to do with the little girl plastered all over the news last night? I was going to make that a priority case first thing."

"Sadly, you've hit the nail on the head. Shocking case. The mother was killed outright when a train struck her."

Maddy winced and closed her eyes. "Thanks, that image is going to live with me for the rest of the day now." Opening her eyes again, she said, "So the mother was killed, and the child abducted, after the event or before?"

"No flies on you. Before. The mother tried to protect the child from being taken but failed. She took a blow to the head, and it would appear she was suffering from concussion when she dipped under the barrier at a level crossing. The train struck before she had a chance to figure out what was happening."

Maddy gasped. "Oh my, that's terrible. That poor woman. Don't tell me the child saw the incident?"

Sara shrugged. "I'm not sure. We have to assume she did. If that's right, then the girl is going to be an emotional wreck. She's probably that already due to her abduction without the added trauma of witnessing her mother's demise. Crap, we need to find her, Maddy, and quickly."

"That much is obvious. How can I help?"

"We need to know if there's some kind of link to the other children who you have registered as abducted. Can you give me a list of their names?"

"I know there's been a spate of them in the last few months. How far back do you want me to go?"

"Say six months. Off the top of your head, can you remember how many have gone missing in the last month or so?"

"Four. The number is imprinted on my mind. Going back six months could take me a while. Do you want me to get back to you later with the information?"

"Please, although if you can give me the names of the four recent ones, that might help to form a picture for now."

Maddy got to work on her keyboard right away, and within seconds the printer churned into action in the corner of the room.

Carla left her seat to collect the information which she handed to Sara.

"Thanks. We'll have to visit the parents at some time or another. What shall I tell them?"

"That we're still doing our best, I suppose. I assume all the officers out there are aware the children are still missing."

"How often do you relay that information, Maddy?"

"Once a week."

"Do you ever get any feedback? Any possible sighting information?" Sara asked.

"Not usually. I know I bleat on about this all the time, but it's worth mentioning again. It was different a few years ago when there were bobbies walking the streets. If they heard a rumour, they were able to check up on it instantly. Nowadays, we're solely reliant on the members of the public to be our eyes and ears for us out there." She shook her head.

"I agree. It's totally wrong. Maybe I can have a word with my DCI, see if we can't change things around a little."

"That would be good. Something needs to alter if we're determined to stay on top of things. This recent clutch of kids going missing, well, anything could have happened to them by now. You're aware the slave trade is growing, right?"

"Unfortunately, yes. It's like living in the dark ages at times."

"We're to blame, the police, I stand by that. We should be out there more, keeping our fingers on the pulse of what's going on in our community."

"I hear you. I know how passionately you feel about this. I promise I'll try and have a word with the DCI by the end of the day."

"I wish someone would. It could mean the difference between these kids living and dying."

There were only so many times Sara could apologise for procedures that she also felt antiquated and needed amending.

"Sorry, it's wrong of me to keep repeating myself. Let me crack on and find the information you've requested and get back to you. I'm sure you have more important tasks to be getting on with than sitting here listening to me whinge on about things."

"Your heart is in the right place, Maddy, that's all that matters to me. I wouldn't class that as whingeing in the slightest. We can hang around for ten minutes, if you can work your magic in that time."

Maddy rolled her eyes. "I know I'm fast, but ten minutes is pushing it. Let's see what I can do for you." Her fingers glided across the keyboard. Every now and then Maddy glanced up from her screen and grinned at them.

Sara discreetly looked at her watch. Time was getting on.

"There we are. Done in record time. Carla, would you do the honours?"

Carla left her seat again, collected another printout and gave it to Sara.

Sara scanned the list of names. Ten in total, four of which appeared on the original list.

"Ten of them. Varying in age from five to nine. What are the chances these kids are all being held together?"

Carla shrugged. "Not sure. I suppose it would be daft not to link them."

"I agree," Maddy said, a frown of frustration pulling at her brow.

"Then that's what we'll do. We'll make this our priority today, Carla. You and I will delve into the cases, seek out the investigating officers and see what we can come up with. Hopefully, it will lead us to these kids. First of all, I'm going to make good on my promise to you, Maddy, and drop by the DCI's office for a quick chat."

"Excellent news. Will you let me know how you get on?"

"Of course. Likewise, if you hear anything, either about the children on the list or any other likely kids who go missing, will you ring me?"

"You have my word on that. In the meantime, I might as well distribute the list I've created for you to the rest of the officers in the area."

"Good for you. It can't hurt keeping these kids' plights fresh in people's minds."

Sara and Carla left the room and descended the stairs again. They split up at the beginning of the next level.

"I won't be long. Why don't you make a start?"

"Good luck with the DCI."

The DCI's secretary, Mary, was busy filing papers away in the cabinet when she entered the room. "Sorry to drop by unannounced. Is she in?"

"Yes, she's in. Knock on the door, I'm sure she'll want to see you, Inspector."

"Thanks, Mary." Sara smiled and crossed the small office. She rapped the door with her knuckle.

"Come in."

Sara opened the door and entered the room. "Do you have five minutes for a chat, boss?"

"Ten minutes at the most. I'm expecting an important call from the super. You look worried, Sara. Anything I can help with?"

She walked towards the chair and sank into it. Crossing one leg over the other, she let out a sigh. "I'm hoping so, ma'am."

"Coffee?"

"Not for me, I'm all coffeed out right now."

"Crikey, I never thought I'd live to hear you utter those words. Come on, spill. What's on your mind?"

"I've just paid a visit to missing persons and promised Maddy I'd have a word with you about something that is puzzling us both."

"Well, get on with it, Inspector. Stop skirting around the issue."

"Okay. A case landed on my desk yesterday—a death and an abduction investigation. The mother died in an incident involving a train while the daughter was abducted."

"Is this the same case that was aired on the news last night?"

"It is."

"What's the problem? Apart from the obvious, of course."

"I'm sure you're aware there's been a number of abductions in the Hereford area recently. The troubling part is that none of these children have been returned to their families yet. Maddy and I were wondering if between us, and with your assistance of course, we could come up with a plan to get our guys out there, where it matters."

DCI Price frowned. "I'm not with you. In what capacity? Oh, wait, you can't mean officers walking the beat?" She wagged her finger.

"That would be the ideal scenario, yes, but I know full well that is never likely to happen again, not with all the cuts in place. I was wondering if we could come up with something between us. It sickens me to think there are people out there willing to strike at a moment's notice and get away with their crimes because we're not able to prevent it."

DCI Price held her hand up and shook her head. "While I agree with you, this has been an age-old problem of ours. You know what the senior bods will say about this, don't you?"

"Yes, I appreciate they'll point out the amount of funding they've put into installing CCTV cameras everywhere and, whilst in most cases they act as a deterrent, there are criminals out there laughing at us."

"Again, that's always been prevalent in our society, Inspector. As far as I'm aware, crime rates are down in this area, am I right?"

"You're right, overall they are down. The problem as I see it is that abductions of kids are way up. Why? I can't tell you that."

DCI Price sank back into her chair and placed her linked hands on the desk. "You believe there's a connection to all these abductions, don't you?"

Sara hitched her shoulders up to meet her ears. "It might be too early to say that, but there's a definite possibility. Carla and I have ten cases we need to go over this morning. We'll be speaking to the other investigating officers and comparing notes. The troubling part is that some of these kids were abducted as long as six months ago. It could be too late for them."

"As in, they might already be dead?"

"Yes. Surely our guys should be out there searching for these children."

"No doubt the investigating officers have done their best, given the funds provided for them."

"Is their *best* good enough?" Sara challenged, her stomach churning itself into knots.

DCI Price chortled. "I wouldn't say that within a few feet of them if I were you. That's a pretty insulting perspective you have there, Inspector."

"I didn't mean it to come across as that, ma'am. I guess I'm frustrated. Let me put it another way. Were you aware that ten children have been abducted in Hereford in the last six months?"

The colour rose in the DCI's cheeks, and she shook her head slowly. "When you put it that way, no, I wasn't fully aware of the problem."

"And yet if I told you how many robberies had taken place in the area in the same time, you'd have a rough idea, right?"

"Yes, around four thousand." Her voice trailed off as if what Sara was highlighting had just sunk in. "I get where you're coming from now. It's shameful that these children are missing still. Let's see what we can do to amend that situation. I'm tasking you with this, Inspector. I want you to report back to me once you've spoken to the other leading investigators on all the cases."

Sara puffed out her cheeks. "I think that will cause problems, if you don't mind me saying, ma'am."

"Why? Because you're still classed as a newbie around here? That's utter nonsense and something I'd like to stamp out right away."

"Possibly. Oh, I don't know. There's the added scenario of me being a female officer."

The DCI slammed upright and smashed a clenched fist onto the desk. "No. You're wrong. I won't allow that, not in this day and age. I've fought hard over the years to ensure women officers are treated fairly by their male counterparts."

"Whoa! Hold your horses there, boss lady, it was just something that flittered through my mind. I'm probably speaking out of turn and doing my male colleagues an injustice on that front. I can't say I've personally come up against anything of that ilk this year."

"Then why on earth mention it, Inspector?"

Sara's mouth pulled down at the sides. "I'm not sure. Ignore me.

Sorry. I'll report back once I've got the lowdown from the officers working the other cases. I really didn't mean to raise an issue that hasn't even surfaced yet. Maybe that was more down to my self-confidence still being a problem now and again."

DCI Price smiled and nodded. "I suppose that's understandable in the circumstances. Just so you know, if you come across any form of sexism in this station, you come to me right away, deal?"

"Yes, boss. You have my word."

The phone on the desk rang. The DCI cringed. "Okay, you better leave now. This is the call I was expecting. Keep in touch on how the case is proceeding."

"I will. Thanks, boss." For some reason, Sara felt the need to tiptoe out of the room as DCI Price answered the phone.

On her journey back to the incident room, her mobile rang. Mark's name showed up in the tiny screen, and joy spread through her and squeezed her heart. She paused and leant against the wall to take the call. "Hello, you. I was going to ring you later."

He laughed softly. "I've saved you a job then. I missed your call last night."

"Sorry, we had an emergency case come in just as I was about to leave for the day. I didn't get home until gone one. I thought about ringing you then but decided it wouldn't be a good idea."

"Crikey! I had no idea you put in those sort of hours. I'm glad you didn't ring. I'm a right grouch when the phone wakes me up."

"That's what I thought. What can I do for you?"

"In other words, you're busy and I'm screwing up your schedule."

"Kind of. I don't wish to appear rude."

"You're not. I was ringing up on the off-chance that you might fancy going out for a drink tonight?"

"I thought we'd arranged to go out at the weekend for dinner."

"We have, but I don't think I can wait until Saturday to see you. It's only Tuesday."

Sara held back a snigger. "Oh gosh, nothing like having a demanding man in your life to keep you on track."

"Demanding? Is that how you see me? Oh dear, have I made a huge mistake ringing you? I'm not stalking you, I promise."

"Oi! Steady on there. I made a flippant remark, that was all. To be honest with you, I think I'm going to be dead on my feet by the time my shift ends tonight. Would you mind if I take a rain check on that one?"

He sighed. "Okay, I suppose I was chancing my arm asking anyway."

A stab of guilt touched her heart. "If you'll let me finish, I was about to suggest that you pop over to my place. I could stop by the supermarket on the way home, pick up a large pizza and a few cans of lager if you fancy it."

"It would be great to see you. I won't be finished here until eight, though. If that's not too late, I could be with you fifteen minutes later. How's that?"

"It sounds like a date to me."

"Brilliant. Can't wait to see you. Bye for now."

"Thanks for ringing, Mark." She hung up. On her walk back to the incident room, a female officer passed her and said, "Morning, boss. You look like the cat that got the cream."

She laughed. "Not yet, but hopefully soon." It was evident how joyful she was to have Mark in her life, but as she'd learnt over the years, being happy always tended to be balanced out with feeling some form of pain. This had made her wary over the years.

Take things slowly. There's no need to spoil things this early on in the relationship. Is that what Mark and I have? A relationship? Or is it considered to be more of a friendship? Yes, we did share a kiss on our last date, but that was all. He'd surprised her by calling. She hadn't expected to hear from him during the week. She was pleased and a little relieved by that.

She would need to set her personal life aside for the rest of the day. She had a little girl in desperate need of her help.

CHAPTER 3

THE MORE THE GIRL SOBBED, the quicker Chris's excitement evaporated. She wasn't like the others. They had all accepted their fate without question through fear. No, he'd realised from the moment he'd abducted her that she would be different. It was unfortunate her mother had died on the track; that hadn't been his intention at all. Maybe that was why the girl was crying all the time. She'd screamed, almost deafening him, when she'd seen her mother struck by the speeding train. None of the other children had been subjected to anything as harsh as that. Perhaps he should learn to be more tolerant in Siobhan's case. Either that or he'd need to slap her around a bit to let her know who was boss.

The rest of the gang didn't have to put up with the crap he had to contend with. It was his choice—he wanted to keep his eye on the kids until the time came around to let them go. It had worked out as planned so far with the others over the past six months. Who knew abducting kids could be so easy and so profitable? When he'd formulated the plan, his intention was to contact the parents for a ransom; however, things hadn't worked out that way. One of his associates had come up with the bright idea of selling the kids. He had the relevant contacts in the underground, meaning the kids could be shifted around easily. To date, five of the eleven girls abducted had been sold and were now living in their permanent homes. He remained in contact until a week after the kids arrived. They were all settled. Whether they were enjoying their new lives or not was something he didn't know or frankly care about. Not a jot.

The money was the driving force behind his actions. His one regret was that he had to share any likely profits he made with the rest of the gang. All right, he took a bigger cut than the rest of them, but a hundred percent would be far better than fifty percent heading his way after every transaction. In all honesty, he had no idea the slave trade was so lucrative. He kicked himself mentally for not getting into all this before. What a waste! All those years of working for others, making them rich beyond their wildest dreams when the opportunity was there all along for him to be living in a grand house, surrounded by its own acreage.

A grin broke out at the thought of how many kids he could take and keep in a grand house. The bigger the house, the more rooms it would likely have, and that meant more money lining his pockets. Was it too late to think along those lines? Was it possible to go it alone? No, the thought had him breaking out in a cold sweat. He was forced to admit that he needed the others. Tory was the one with the underground contacts. Mick and Fran had their uses, too, in regard to feeding the kids. Fran showed her motherly side now and again; she also revealed another side that he hadn't expected to witness. An evilness he hadn't seen since his childhood. His own mother had beaten him if he'd ever dared to say a word out of place. She'd ruled the household with a firm hand after his father had walked out on them when Chris was five.

Up until that point, his mother had been bearable. The second his father had packed his bags and left the house, all his mother's pent-up frustration appeared to be directed at Chris. She'd beaten him night and day for seven solid days on the trot, only feeding him on scraps, while his other two siblings sat at the table with her and went about their lives normally. What hurt him the most was that neither of his sisters stuck up for him. Not a single frigging word left their lips. He pleaded with them using his eyes during numerous beatings, but both Jessica and Fiona had turned their backs on him, in more ways than one. That had broken him, destroyed his heart into thousands of pieces. He was alone, the only male in the house expected to stand there without uttering a word and take the punishment meted out to him.

Siobhan's sobs tightened his muscles and grated on his nerves as the old memories came back to haunt him. Memories he'd successfully buried for years. *Why doesn't she just shut up and accept her fate like the other kids did?*

Fran and Mick Granger arrived at the house at around eleven. En route, Fran had picked up several doughnuts from the baker's in the high street. She said it made the kids more compliant if she treated them now and again to sugary things.

"Wow, she's got some lungs on her. What's her problem?" Fran asked, looking over at the girl tied to the bed in the corner of the room. Luckily, the house was detached and situated at the end of a lane that led out into the country. Passers-by were rare, especially at this time of the year.

He shrugged and lowered his voice. "Her mother got killed in front of her. At least I think that's her problem."

Fran checked on the girl and walked back to him. She swiped his arm. "Bloody idiot! She's in pain. Look at the angle her wrist is at. It's bloody broken."

"Doh! Well, you're the damned nurse. See to it and stop having a go at me. I did the best I could in the circumstances. Where's Tory? Have you guys seen him?"

Fran tutted and made her way back to the girl, talking soothingly to the scared wretch. At last the girl's sobs subsided into something far more acceptable for him to cope with. Mick sat in a chair at the table and got out his phone. He was forever trawling through his Facebook page or checking his damn emails as if he was someone important. He wasn't. Chris could do away with these two if he desired. It would be easy to cut them out of a deal at any given time if he wanted to. He didn't. He needed them as much as they needed him. Correction, as much as they needed the money involved in this gig. Still, Fran had her uses with the kids. She was an ex-nurse. Her caring side showed up when it was required, but more often than not, she watched over the kids with an eye of a headmistress who just about tolerated kids.

"Is anyone going to answer me?" Chris kicked out at Mick's shoe to gain his attention.

"Hey, don't take your fucking foul mood out on me, mate. No, we ain't seen him."

"Calm down, the pair of you," Fran called over her shoulder. "He was due to have a meeting with his associate, you know the one," she replied, skirting around the inference that his associate was the man who was responsible for taking the kids off their hands.

"Yeah, I thought he was due to meet him today. I suppose he'll show up here later if he has any news. What have you two been up to?" Chris asked.

"What we discussed. I've been out there sourcing more mopeds, ready for the next part of our plan," Mick said.

Chris scratched the side of his face. "I've been thinking about that."

"Oh crap, here it comes. Every time you say that the frigging plan changes. What's wrong now?" Mick slammed his phone onto the table, then must have regretted his actions and checked he hadn't damaged the screen.

"Well, after what happened yesterday, I don't think mopeds are the way to go. I thought they would be the best way for us to get away from a crime scene, but I was wrong. They're too slow."

Mick scraped his chair on the wooden floor and faced him. He prodded him in the chest with his chubby finger. "That's frigging great, and you're just telling me now? The thought didn't cross your mind to mention it yesterday? You're such a pain in the arse at times, man. You're unbelievable."

"I'm sorry. What more can I say? Mistakes happen. It's better to say it now than use the mopeds and get caught in the act."

"Boys, pack it in or you'll start her off again. Take your argument outside," Fran hissed at them.

"I ain't going nowhere," her husband, Mick, said. He folded his arms across his large stomach in defiance.

The only thing running through Chris's head at that moment was how he could kill Mick. He'd always been an annoyance, right from the start. Instead, Chris shrugged and smiled at the man. "All right, if everything is in place, we'll do it your way." Then he joked, "The mopeds better be of the robust variety if they have to withstand your weight."

Mick narrowed his eyes and took a step towards him.

Chris held up his hands and retreated. "What's the matter, can't you take a joke?"

"Maybe I've been around you too long. You're enough to try any man's patience the way you sprout these ideas then change your mind halfway through. It's gotta stop. You're driving us all nuts, take my word on that."

"Oh, I am, am I? Maybe we should call off our partnership then. Oh, wait, no, you greedy fuckers want the money as much as I do. So back off, shitface."

Mick growled and stepped closer.

Fran issued them both a hissed warning again, "Mick, you dare, and you'll have me to contend with. Sit down. Both of you think of what you're saying in front of the girl."

Siobhan sobbed loudly.

The noise grated on Chris's nerves for the umpteenth time that day. "Shut her up, for fuck's sake!"

"Lower your voice and stop swearing or I'll come over there and give you a broken nose," Fran warned with a piercing glare.

"Too late. My own mother did that years ago. Nothing you could do to me will outdo anything she did, I promise you that."

The room fell silent. Even Siobhan's sobs dried up as Fran made a splint for her wrist. When she'd settled the girl down on the bed, Fran returned to Mick and Chris.

She put her hand on Chris's shoulder and squeezed. "We're all sorry for what you went through, Chris, but you're going to have to keep that sour-grapes attitude reined in. Think of what we've achieved so far. We're building up to the main target now, right? That should improve your mood when you get your reward. But you're going to need us all with you to achieve your aim, so stop dishing out the crap and start learning to pull with us and not against us. Otherwise, things are likely to go belly up. That's a promise and not a threat, by the way."

Seething inside at being told there was a likelihood things wouldn't work out the way he'd planned, he took a step back and turned away from the husband and wife before he conceded, "All right. I promise to stop shooting my mouth off. We're going to need to have a proper chat when Tory gets here though, agreed?" he asked, facing them again.

As if he'd summoned him up, the fourth member of the gang entered the lounge. He wore a smug grin and threw himself into one of the chairs around the table, stretched out his legs in front of him and placed his hands behind his head. "That was a pretty successful morning. How about you guys?"

"Mick's managed to sort out the mopeds, and Fran has successfully shut the kid up," Chris replied before either of the others could speak.

"Yeah, and smartarse here informed us that he's changed his mind about the mopeds," Mick grumbled disapprovingly.

"What? You're crazy, Chris. We have to stick with the plan we all agreed on. You can't alter it if it no longer appeals to you."

"I'm not altering things intentionally. None of us have used mopeds before yesterday. All I'm doing is giving you guys some feedback."

"Feedback we should have received yesterday," Mick insisted grumpily.

Chris threw his arms up in the air. They came crashing down and slammed against his thighs. "All right, we've just covered this, there's no need to go over things again."

Mick pointed at Tory. "There is. He wasn't here."

Fran tutted, but it was Tory who spoke next. "Guys, if you're gonna fall out over trivial matters like this, we might as well call it a day now."

"*Trivial matters?* Hardly, mate. Mopeds are slow. I should know. Anyone could have caught me during the getaway yesterday. Thank fuck the cops weren't around. All I'm doing is trying to safeguard our future plans. If you lot aren't willing to listen to me, then our downfall will be on your heads, not mine."

"Ever the fucking drama queen, Chris. Grow some balls, will you? We agreed from the outset that mopeds were the way to go. You'll simply have to be more inventive when leaving a crime scene. Take an alternative route down an alley for instance, somewhere a car can't follow you. Do I really have to be the one to spell things out for you? I thought you had a brain in that head of yours." Tory glared at him.

Chris curled his lip. "That's below the belt, Tory, even for you. I've had enough for one day. I need a break from you lot." He stormed out of the room and through the front door of the house, knowing full well the three of them would have the knives out the minute he returned, if only figuratively speaking.

He wandered up and down the road, kicking out at the stones lying in his path as he thought. Thirty minutes dragged by before he contemplated returning to the house. He walked into the room, and the three others stopped talking. He glanced over at the girl on the bed, thankful she was asleep at last.

"I know my name is probably mud, but guys, you need to take on board what I'm telling you," he said, keen to fight his corner.

"And you need to hear our point of view and stop throwing a temper tantrum when someone objects to what you say. The plan was discussed at length. We're too far down the road to alter things now, Chris. Accept it for what it is and move on," Tory said, his left eye twitching in anger.

Chris knew for the plan to work and for a peaceful life, he'd have to accept the way things were. *I'll be the first to throw around the accusations after everything is complete.* "Hey, okay, that's fine by me. I thought the feedback would come in handy. If you guys want to ignore it, that's your lookout."

The other three glared at him. It was the first time any of them had spoken out against the others. He could sense the dynamics changing within the team. Something he'd be wary about going forward, during the next job they had planned.

CHAPTER 4

THE DAY PROVED to be a frustrating one for Sara and her team. Yes, they'd received a few calls from the general public, some of them irate that the man had been seen with a child on a moped, but not one of those people intimated they knew where the moped was now. They'd all seen the bike en route to somewhere, but there was nothing definitive there either.

At six o'clock, Sara ordered the team to go home and get some rest. They all seemed as deflated as she was when they made their way out of the office. Sara sighed, collected her coat and switched off the light in her office. She was just leaving the station when the desk sergeant stopped her. She inclined her head as she listened to his side of the conversation while he was on the phone.

After a few seconds he hung up. His gaze meeting hers, he said, "I think this could be of interest to you, boss."

"What's that, Jeff? Can it possibly wait until the morning? I'm pooped."

"I dare say it could, boss. I'll let you decide that. Around twenty minutes ago, a woman was attacked as she walked home from work."

"Where? Not sure how this concerns me. People are attacked every day, aren't they?"

"In Broad Street, the centre of town. The thing that struck me is that the woman was attacked by someone on a moped."

"Crap! Now I see where this is leading. Damn, the team have all left for the evening. I really don't want to call them back in after doing extra hours yesterday. Is the woman all right?"

"She's been rushed to hospital. The bastard threw acid in her face."

"Shit! Why?" She waved a hand in front of her. "Don't answer that. I'll get over to A&E now, see what I can find out." She glanced at the clock on the wall. The hospital was close to Morrisons anyway, so she could still pick up the pizza and lager as well as slot in a visit to the victim. "Thanks, Jeff. See you in the morning, unless something else develops overnight. Call me if you come across anything else you think might be linked."

"I will, boss. Sorry to spoil your evening like this."

"You haven't, don't worry about it." She rushed across the car park, jumped in her vehicle and sped away from the station.

The hospital was within spitting distance. She waited patiently in a queue at the traffic lights, drumming her fingers on the steering wheel. A sudden chill touched her spine, so she switched on the car heater and sighed a little when the heat hit her face. Ten minutes later, she found a parking spot in the hospital car park, placed a card on the dashboard to let the parking attendant know that she was an officer on duty and raced through the front door.

The signs led her to A&E where she showed her ID to the young woman on reception. "DI Sara Ramsey. I was informed that a woman had come in, suspected acid attack."

"Ah, yes. If you'd care to take a seat, I'll get one of the nursing staff to come and see you."

The receptionist hadn't left her seat long when a scream erupted from behind the swing doors at the end of the corridor. Drawn to the woman's anxiety, Sara walked towards the door. The receptionist emerged, surprised to see her standing there.

"Someone will be out to explain what's happening soon."

"Thank you. I take it the scream was from the woman involved in the attack?"

"It was. She's in a sorry state. Never seen anything like it, not around here anyway."

Sara nodded and issued the woman an understanding smile. She paced the area until a male came through the doors a few minutes later. "Are you the policewoman?"

"Yes, DI Sara Ramsey, Doctor."

He walked a few feet up the hallway and turned to face her. "The patient is doing well. We believe we've removed all the acid. As you can imagine, the damage is considerable. Her face took the full impact of the attack. At a guess I'd say she has at least ninety-five percent burns."

Bile rose in her throat. She swallowed it back down and asked, "What happens next?"

"Nothing. The wound will take time to heal. Hopefully we've managed to prevent the acid from burning its way deeper through the skin layers and into her bloodstream. That's not to say the damage is any less. I'm only saying this so you can prepare yourself. Our stomachs are hardened to injuries such as this."

"Thanks, Doc. Can I see her now?"

"We're going to transfer her to one of the side wards first. We'll keep her nearby for now, easier to check on her regularly."

"I'll wait here then, if that's okay?"

"I'd suggest either waiting in the reception area or the family waiting room up there." He pointed to the end of the corridor. "It could take us another thirty minutes or so to move her."

"That's okay. I'm not in a rush." She walked slowly up the hallway, glancing at the crayoned pictures on the wall, obviously drawn by children possibly while they waited for news of a loved one. Once seated, she flicked through a couple of magazines, staring at the photos of beautifully designed houses, her envy gene suppressed for a change because of the incident and her surroundings. After a few minutes, she decided to ring Mark on his mobile.

"Hi, don't tell me you're calling off our date," he answered the phone, sounding upset.

"No, although I am ringing up to tell you that I'm sitting in the waiting room at the hospital at present. Hopefully I'll be home by eight. Just wanted to let you know in case you got worried."

"Anything wrong?"

"No, at least not with me. I had to come. It's another attack which I think could be related to an ongoing case. I can't go into any more detail than that, sorry."

"I understand. If you'd rather postpone tonight, I'll be fine either way."

"No, please. I'm sure I won't be here long once I've spoken to the woman. She'll need her rest, too. I'm sure they have her dosed up against the pain."

"No doubt about that. Okay, I'll see you later. Are you sure you don't want me to pick up a takeaway instead?"

"Go on then, you've twisted my arm. Anything you select is fine by me. As long as you let me pay for it."

"We'll argue about that part later. I'll pick up a curry then. Korma all right for you?"

"Perfect. Thanks, Mark. You're one in a million."

"I am indeed. Oops, that came out as me being conceited. I didn't mean it that way."

"Don't be such an idiot. Go, see you soon."

She was still smiling a few seconds later when the doctor poked his head around the door. "We're ready for you now."

Sara left her seat as if flames were lashing at her backside. "How is she?" she asked, trotting to catch up with the young doctor's long strides.

"As you can imagine, she's beside herself."

"Understandable. The pain must've been dreadful as well as the shock involved in such a brutal and obscene attack."

"We've given her something for the pain and to help her sleep, so I'm not entirely sure how lucid she will be, or for how long. Please take that on board when you start questioning her."

"I will, don't worry."

The doctor pulled back the curtain a few inches and stepped through the gap. Sara followed. She'd prepared herself so she didn't gasp when she saw the victim, but nothing could have prepared her for what she saw. She plastered a slight smile in place and introduced herself.

"Hello, Angela. I'm Detective Inspector Sara Ramsey. Are you up to telling me what happened?"

The victim was in her thirties, slim with longish red hair. Her head was resting back on the pillows propped up against the metal head-board. She lifted her head slightly to look at her. "A man attacked me. I was walking home, minding my own bloody business."

"I'm so sorry this happened to you. Can you describe the man? Did he say anything during the attack?"

"He was wearing a helmet, so no, I couldn't see his face. He shouted that I deserved what I got. I have no idea what he was talking about." She pointed a shaking finger at her face. "Do people seriously think that another person deserves to be disfigured like this? I wouldn't wish this on my worst enemy."

"Neither would I. I know it's easy for me to say but I wouldn't take it personally. By that I mean I would regard this as a random attack if you haven't got a clue who could be capable of doing such a thing."

"I haven't. They would have been better off killing me. How am I going to cope? I haven't seen the effects of what he's done yet, but I've seen the damage acid can do to a person's skin. I might as well be dead now. My life is over."

The doctor placed a comforting hand on Angela's arm. "It's amazing what plastic surgeons can do nowadays. You mustn't give up hope, Miss Guppy."

She shook her head as tears dripped onto her inflamed cheeks. "But that will mean undergoing months of painful operations. I don't have it in me to do that. Doctor, you have my permission to give me a huge dose of something that will end it all. I have nothing left to live for."

"Please, Angela, don't say that. Modern day science is remarkable," Sara insisted, siding with the doctor.

Angela's sore eyelids fluttered shut and flew open again. "I'm sleepy. Ask me what you want and then I'd like you to leave."

"Okay, only a few more questions. Were you alone? Or did someone else witness the attack?"

"I work in a solicitor's office. My colleagues were all walking ahead of me. I was lagging behind because I'm in charge of locking up the office when we leave. That's when the attack occurred. I didn't see the man approach; I was distracted, putting the keys away in my handbag. To be honest, I didn't know what had happened at first, not until a couple of my colleagues screamed and rushed to help me. I collapsed onto the ground once the burning began. A few of my friends emptied their bottled water on my face once I started shouting that my face was on fire. I heard another friend ring for the ambulance. I clawed at my skin." She looked down and turned her hands over to study the state of them.

"They'll heal quickly," the doctor announced before Angela had the chance to ask the obvious question.

"Unlike my face," she added tearfully. She swept a clump of hair back from her forehead and screamed when the strands fell away and ended up in her hand. "Oh my God, will I lose all my hair?"

"Not all of it. It's inevitable you will lose some around your forehead. I'm sorry, Miss Guppy," the doctor replied quietly.

"You're not the only one," she sobbed. "Leave me alone. I don't want to talk any more or see anyone. I want to sleep, forget the trauma I've been through."

The doctor glanced at Sara, and they both nodded.

"I'll be back to check on you in a few days, Angela. Please, stay strong," Sara said with a warm smile.

"Stay strong! You have no idea how weak and dejected I feel right now, Inspector. You should be out there looking for the maniac who did this to me, not offering me your wasted words of regret."

"I'm sorry. I have instructed every officer in the area to be on alert for the suspect. That's all we can do at this point."

Angela harrumphed and turned her back on them. Sara led the way back into the corridor. The doctor placed a finger to his lips and steered her a few feet away before he spoke. "It's best if we leave her alone for the rest of the evening. She'll be asleep soon."

"Thank you for letting me see her. We don't have much to go on, but it's better than nothing."

"I must get on; it's a busy evening for us. Please, do your best for her, Inspector. She's going to have to live the rest of her life dealing with the scars of what happened this evening. No amount of plastic surgery will be able to cover the internal scars of what she's going to have to go through in the coming months or years. She deserves justice."

"I appreciate that, Doctor. I intend to make sure she gets the justice she deserves. I can't even pretend to understand what is going on in her head right now. By what she said in there, I think you'll need to keep a close eye on her."

"Don't worry, we will. I'll get one of the burns counsellors to pay her a visit in the next few days. They'll talk her down from being on the brink. They're trained to do that to patients."

"I'll be off then. Can I leave you my card? All right if I leave you two? Perhaps you can give one to Angela once she's had a good night's sleep."

"I will. Good luck with your investigation. I hope for our sakes this doesn't turn out to be the start of something big. More attacks of this ilk...we're understaffed as it is."

Sara held up her crossed fingers. "We're in the same predicament. Thanks for sparing me the time, Doc."

She watched him walk away from her and then returned to the car. It was seven thirty-five—twenty minutes to get home. She wasn't expecting Mark until eight-thirty. He'd probably ring up for the take-away before he left work. That would give her enough time to get home, place a bottle of wine in the fridge and to slip into something more comfortable.

THE LIGHTS of Mark's car shone through the lounge window the second she sat down for a cuddle with Misty. "No rest for the wicked."

She opened the front door to welcome him. She'd put on her lilac velour lounge suit.

He smiled, and his gaze drifted down the length of her slim body. Leaning forward, he kissed her on the cheek. "You made it home then?"

"Only been in about twenty minutes. I could have picked up a pizza and cooked it after all."

"Never mind. I'm famished. The smell of this curry in the car has been so tempting, my tummy is sore from all the agonised pleas to feed it."

Sara laughed and drifted into the kitchen. She switched off the oven, opened the door and removed the warmed plates. "I'm all prepared. Do you want to pour the wine while I dish up? I don't trust your portion control."

"Damn, really? Okay, is the wine in the fridge?"

"Second shelf. Wow, look at this feast. You bought naans as well as rice."

"I know. I thought I'd spoil us, and yes, I'm paying. You can put towards the meal on Saturday if you really want to. I know how independent you are."

"Glad I don't have to repeat myself all the time. I think women should pay their way in this life. Bloody hell, we fought long and hard for equality, right?"

His head tilted side to side. "To an extent I agree with you. Such as salary, there is no need for men to still be pulling in the higher wage; however, I still belong to the old school where paying the bill in a restaurant is concerned."

"You're nuts. Mind you, I don't think there are many kind-hearted men around these days. Philip thought the same as you." She paused after mentioning her dead husband's name. She rarely did that in Mark's company. Maybe it was a sign of how relaxed she was with him.

He took a step towards her and rested his chin on her shoulder. "It's all right to talk about him, I don't mind. We've all got a past, Sara."

Dislodging his chin, she swivelled to face him and placed her arms around his neck, surprising them both, going by the expression on his face. "I know. The last thing I want to do is keep slinging his name in your face, though."

He kissed the tip of her nose. "You're hardly guilty of that. Please, I'm saying this now. Don't ever feel you have to suppress your feelings. You loved Philip and was devastated by his death. I saw how much that had crushed you the day you brought Misty into the surgery after she was poisoned. You told me then that you couldn't lose her as she was a gift from Philip. I saw the way your eyes lit up when you spoke about him—they still do. I don't ever want you to change in that respect. I also appreciate that a part of you possibly died the day he lost his life. If I can furnish you with fifty percent of the happiness you shared with him, it will make me exceptionally happy."

Tears pricked, and Sara struggled to hold them back. This man was special, very much like Philip. There was something standing in her way, not allowing her to fully commit to him, though, and she had no idea what it was. She pecked him on the lips and smiled, then released her arms from around his neck and got back to serving up the dinner.

Mark accepted her reaction and didn't challenge it in the slightest. He efficiently opened the bottle of wine and poured two glasses then placed the bottle back in the fridge. Sara served up the curry. She could tell immediately which was the korma, although it didn't stop her dipping a finger in Mark's curry to taste his.

"Hey, I saw that. You like it?"

"Yummy. What is it?" she replied, running her tongue around her mouth.

He laughed. "Chicken jalfrezi. I don't mind sharing it. I love a korma now and then."

"Deal. I tend to stick with the same dish all the time. It would be good to have other options in the future."

"Bagsy having the keema naan, though. Oh, go on, we could split that as well if you really want to."

"No, that's fine. You can have that. I think my waistline will be stretched to the limit as it is anyway with the curry and the rice. I might have a little nibble if you're feeling generous."

"All right then, if you must."

They took their bulging plates through to the lounge and sat next to each other on the couch. "I recorded *Game of Thrones* if you want to see it."

Mark almost choked on the mouthful of food he'd just started chewing. "Blimey! You do know how gory that programme can be at times, don't you?"

Sara grimaced. "Sorry, forgot about that. Maybe it would be best to save it until after we've finished. Are you up to date on the series?"

"I think so. Sad this is going to be the final season. It took me a few episodes to get into it. Too much sex for my liking in the first few episodes, spoilt the story for me really. Umm...not that I'm a prude."

Sara giggled. "Actually, I agree with you. It didn't add to the story at all. They could've easily left those parts out. Not that I'm a prude either."

They both laughed and clinked their glasses together then tucked into their curries again.

After ten minutes or so, Sara finally placed her fork down on the plate, defeated. "Enough is enough. Glad I'm wearing an elastic waistband."

"I see you ate both the curries. I think I'll leave some of my rice, too. It was a huge portion."

Sara took the plates into the kitchen, scraped the remains in the bin and ran some water in the sink, leaving them to soak overnight. She'd deal with them in the morning or tomorrow night after work, whichever took her fancy more. Then she removed the bottle of wine from the fridge and returned to the lounge to find Mark stroking Misty with one hand while setting up the next episode of *Game of Thrones* with the other. She smiled. He looked at home, but then she paused in the doorway.

Too at home some would say. Would I be one of those people? He's harmless enough. Never given me cause to doubt him as a person. So what's the problem? Time, that's the problem. It's barely been two years since Philip's death.

He glanced up and caught her staring at him. "Something wrong? You've gone really pale."

She shook her head and continued to her seat, placing the bottle of wine on the floor beside her. "Nothing, I'm fine. It's a little cold out there compared to in here, I suppose." *Liar!*

"I've set it up. Hope that's all right? I hate to sit around doing nothing when someone else is busy clearing up."

"Glad to hear it. You and Misty appear to be getting on well." She opened the wine and topped up both of their glasses.

A few hours later, after they'd finished watching the episodes Sara had recorded, they switched off the TV and chatted until finally it was time to draw the evening to a close. Sara gasped. "Oh God, I can't let you drive home after plying you with drink all evening. You better stay over."

Mark's smile was awkward. "Are you sure?"

She couldn't tell if there was a sudden sparkle in his eye or if it was a case of the overhead light glinting in their depths. She cleared her throat. "I haven't got around to buying another bed for the spare room, so it'll have to be the couch if that's okay?"

He chuckled. "Sounds good to me. I really wasn't expecting anything else, I promise."

She was tempted to let out a relieved sigh but was unsure how he'd take that. "Thanks for understanding." She placed the palm of her hand on his cheek.

He closed his eyes and rubbed his face up and down, enjoying her touch. Her stomach clenched. The motion felt good, but again, there was something holding her back. She snatched her hand away and jumped out of her seat. "I'll go and get the spare quilt."

"Glad to hear you've got one," Mark replied, appearing at ease with the situation even if she wasn't.

Sara ran up the stairs, sourced the quilt, a spare pillow and a set of bedding and dressed the items, all the time kicking herself for being an emotional wreck, dithering about what to do next for the best.

Hard to believe I'm so assertive at work and yet that assertiveness abandons me once I leave the station. After giving herself a good talking to, she returned to the lounge. "There you are. That should keep you warm for the night. According to the weatherman, the temperatures are going to start dropping overnight now."

"If I get too cold I'm sure Misty will warm me up." He pointed at the cat making itself at home on his fresh bedding.

Sara laughed and picked Misty up. "Hey, cheeky, you're sleeping with me tonight, as usual. I'll just put her out for a minute and then go up. Do you need anything else, Mark?"

His piercing gaze met hers, and time stood still for a moment. "Only a goodnight kiss, if it's not too much trouble."

Sara took a couple of small steps towards him, her heart rate increasing with each step. They shared the simplest of kisses and then parted. "Can I get you a hot drink?"

"No, I'm fine. All right if I use the bathroom?"

"Sure. There's a fresh towel in the cupboard, and if you look in the bathroom cabinet, I think you'll find a new toothbrush. I was due to change mine soon. I can pick up a new one when I go shopping next."

"Wow, you're super organised. I guess I'm a typical male in that respect."

Sara shrugged. "I've never thought about it before." She went out into the kitchen to let Misty out. While she waited for her cat to return, she decided to wash the dishes after all but left them to drain overnight. Misty walked through the back door and immediately headed for her bowl. Sara sprinkled in some dried food and locked the back door. She heard Mark coming down the stairs.

He popped his head around the doorframe. "I'll say goodnight then, Sara. Thank you for a wonderful, relaxing evening."

"It was fun. Sleep well, Mark. You might want to close the door to prevent any unwanted visitors during the night." Her cheeks flared up, and she blustered. "By that I meant Misty."

He laughed. "I know what you meant." He turned his back and muttered something else that sounded to her ear like, "Although I wouldn't mind if it was you."

She chose not to say anything. After Misty had finished her meal, Sara checked the front door was locked—force of habit after Misty had been poisoned—and then made her way up to bed. She was shocked to see the time on her bedside clock: five minutes to one. "Crikey, I hope I can sleep. I have a feeling I'm going to be fit for nothing in the morning."

CHAPTER 5

SARA HAD FINALLY DRIFTED off around three. She'd found it impossible to sleep, aware that Mark was in the house. Why? Well, she was still trying to figure out that part. She showered and dressed before venturing downstairs to find Mark already dressed in the kitchen.

"Good morning," he said brightly, extra stubble on his chin. "Fancy a cuppa? Or do you have to shoot off?"

Sara glanced at her watch. It was only seven-thirty; she had time for a quick one. "Go on then. Do you want some toast? I think I have half a loaf of bread still."

"Maybe a slice, just to keep the hunger at bay. Sleep well?"

She placed two slices of bread in the toaster. "I should be asking you that."

"I don't even remember turning the light out. I slept right through until I heard you moving about."

"Sorry. I tried to be quiet. What time do you usually surface in the morning?"

"About seven, it's fine. I hope this doesn't sound bad, but you look rough."

Sara chuckled. "Gee, thanks. I couldn't sleep for some reason. I get like that sometimes in the middle of a case."

"I wondered if it was that. Not sure I could do your job."

The toast popped up. "You get used to it most of the time. Butter or marmalade?"

"Butter for me, please. Out of curiosity, does sleep come easier once you've caught a suspect?"

"Oh yes. I can generally sleep ten hours straight."

"Wow. Is it the same for all coppers or are you the exception?"

"I couldn't tell you, it's not something we discuss at work. I suppose it's dedication to the job that keeps me awake. You must go through the same being a vet, surely?"

"My sleep has never suffered. I do get wound up during the day if an animal doesn't respond as expected to the treatment." He bit into his toast and then took a sip of coffee.

"Right, I better finish this and make a move. There's no need for you to rush. I'll give you the spare key and you can lock up when you leave."

"You'd trust me with your key?" he asked, surprised.

"Of course. Are you telling me that I shouldn't?"

"No, not at all. I'd rather not, if it's all the same. I'll leave when you do. Will Misty be okay during the day?"

"Yep. I'll quickly change her litter tray before I go. She'll be fine. I keep her indoors while I'm at work, mainly because there's still heavy plant equipment being used on site. Not long to go now before the builders complete the houses around here."

They finished the rest of their breakfast. Mark washed up while Sara cleaned Misty's tray and refreshed the litter. She made a fuss of Misty for a second or two, then she and Mark left the house together.

"What the...?" Mark shouted as they got closer to his car.

Sara gasped when she saw the state of his vehicle. "Who would do such a thing?"

The whole side of his Suzuki Jeep was missing the paintwork.

"Someone has used bloody paint stripper by the looks of it."

"Crap. Why?" Sara's mind was suddenly swept up in a tornado. A few months ago, when Misty had been poisoned, she'd also received a threatening text. She searched around her. *Is someone out there watching me? They must be. Why else would they target Mark's car? The bastards! Who the hell are you? If I get my hands on you...*

"You need to report this as an act of vandalism, Mark. I feel so guilty."

"Why should you feel guilty?" He looked up and down the road. There was no one in sight. "I reckon whoever did this is long gone. Maybe they did it last night before we went to bed."

"I think you're right. I'm going to call it in. Get a squad car out here."

"You'll be wasting your time. The culprit will be long gone. I'll drop by the station during the day. Don't worry about it, Sara, you have enough on your plate right now."

"I'll still mention it. Ask at the station, see if there have been any other incidents of this nature around this area. It's not something I'm familiar with, different department and all that. I'm so sorry this has happened to you. Let me pay towards the repairs."

"Nonsense. I couldn't let you do that. I'm sure the insurance will cover it. Actually, I'm not sure they will. I've got a mate in the trade, he'll see me right. Damn, it's the inconvenience more than anything. I was due to go to Birmingham on a two-day course in a few days."

"Bollocks, you'll have to hire a car. I'd offer you mine to use but I need it."

He waved away her suggestion. "No bother. Again, my mate will see me right. I'm sure he'll have an old banger lying around I can use." He shrugged. "Right, enough of this doom and gloom. There's nothing we can do about it, so we might as well move on. Thanks again for a lovely evening. Would it be all right if I ring you tonight?"

She leant forward and pecked him on the cheek. "I'd feel disappointed if you didn't. Good luck. Let me know how you get on."

"Thanks. Talk later then. Have a good day. At least mine can't get any worse," he said, forcing a smile.

Feeling despondent, Sara got in her car and drove into work. Mark followed her a quarter of the way before he turned off. He flashed her, and she waved. After parking in her designated spot at the station, she walked through the main entrance and stopped at the reception area to speak to Jeff. "Morning, Jeff. I've got a bit of a problem."

"Oh, anything I can help with, boss?"

"I'm hoping so. A friend of mine had his car vandalised during the night. Some bastard used paint stripper on his Jeep."

Jeff winced. "Ouch. There was a spate of that going on back when I used to be on the beat, usually connected to gang members if I recall. Not seen the like of it since then."

"Interesting. My train of thought is that the incident might be connected to the case we're working at present. It's a long shot, I know. My friend will be contacting the station later to report it. Can you do me a favour and try and give him some words of encouragement that the vandalism will be investigated?"

"Of course, boss. I'll treat him as if he's one of our own. What's his name?"

"Thanks, Jeff. It's Mark Fisher. Will you dig through the database, see if any other crimes of this nature have been reported in, say, the last six months?"

"I will do. Nothing is coming to mind, but that doesn't mean a thing. The crime might have been reported and not dealt with. You know how strapped we are regarding similar crimes to this."

"That's what's worrying me. How many times over the years have we seen crimes like this lead to far worse ones? Criminals test the waters all the time, you know that as well as I do."

"Yep. If only the government allowed us the proper resources to deal with the scallywags intent on doing this kind of damage."

"I know. I reckon it would make our lives a lot easier in the long run, right?"

"You took the words out of my mouth, boss."

"I better get on. All quiet around here last night I take it?"

"As far as I know. Only started thirty minutes ago myself. I'll have a shufty through the notes and get back to you if anything important crops up."

"If I don't hear from you within the next twenty minutes, I'll take it as read, we're in the clear." Sara ascended the stairs to the incident room and switched on the lights then bypassed the vending machine to go directly to her office. She groaned inwardly when she saw the pile of brown envelopes awaiting her arrival. "They can wait, I'm definitely not in the mood for that crap today." Depositing her bag and coat on the rack, she left the office again and walked over to the whiteboard to study the information the team had added about the case. Once she'd refreshed her mind, she picked up the marker and wrote Angela Guppy's name in capital letters on the left-hand side. She took a step back and heard a noise behind her.

"Morning, boss," Carla said, cheerily dropping her bag by her desk and slipping off her jacket. "Everything all right?"

"Morning, Carla, not really. I'd rather tell you all together if that's all right. I do have something I want to share with you, though."

"Coffee?" Carla asked, already on her way to the machine.

"Please." Sara waited for her partner to join her, took a sip of coffee.

Carla leant in closer. "This looks ominous. Have I done something wrong?"

"No, don't be daft. This is personal. I'd rather keep it between you and me for now, okay?"

Carla nodded and perched on the desk behind her.

"You remember the incident with my cat several months ago?"

"Yeah, how could I forget? Oh God, it hasn't happened again, has it?"

"No, Misty is unharmed but..." She paused. Ever the one to keep her personal life just that, personal, she wondered if she was doing the right thing revealing the truth to a colleague about Mark. Was she ready for that? *Sod it! I have to tell her. I can't have this weighing me down. She'll know something is bothering me and probably end up thinking it's something she's done.*

"But? You're worrying me. Just say it, boss. The others will be here soon."

She has a point. Get on with it. "Okay, I've been seeing someone. A man."

63

"That's good to know. I wasn't under the impression you'd swapped sides."

Sara pulled a face. "Ever the comedian. Anyway, he stayed over last night." She raised a hand when Carla opened her mouth to speak. "On the couch, nothing naughty, I promise."

"Why not? You're entitled to have a bit of fun. I'm sure Philip would agree with me on that score. Oh, wait, you don't think he's still around you, watching your every move, do you?"

Sara shook her head. "I know you're pulling my leg when you say that; however, sometimes, that's exactly how I feel. Unless you've lost someone dear to you as I have, you can't possibly know what I'm going through. Sorry, I didn't mean to snap. What am I doing? You don't want to hear this shit."

Carla reached out a hand and touched her arm. "Please, Sara, I want to understand. I want to be someone you feel you can open up to. I wasn't being flippant, I swear. I'm genuinely interested in how you feel, the kind of sensations you get when you're at home, alone in your house, except you weren't, were you? Now I'm waffling."

Sara chortled. "All right. One day I'll open up about that side of things, I promise, just not today. I have more important things to worry about." She lowered her voice again to say the next part. "Mark's car was vandalised overnight."

Carla's eyes widened, and her mouth formed a large circle. "Whoa! Seriously? In what way?"

"Someone poured paint stripper down the side. He's devastated. I tried to put it down to a one-off incident, but up here," she added, jabbing a finger against her forehead, "I can't do that. Something is going on. First Misty, then the text, now this."

"What? What bloody text? You haven't told me about that."

Sara sighed, and her shoulders slumped. "I didn't think anything of it." She withdrew her phone and scrolled through the texts then handed it to Carla.

"Jesus. Someone goes out of their way to tell you that poisoning your cat was nothing compared to what they're going to do to you, and you choose to ignore it? You're insane. Actually, your logic is way off the mark. If it didn't bother you, then why on earth would you keep the text?"

"I don't know. There hasn't been anything since the poisoning. I thought they'd made their point and were now leaving me alone. I'm having to rethink that notion now that Mark's car has been vandalised."

"What if that's a coincidence?" Carla asked, looking puzzled.

"I've thought about that, but I live on a new estate way out in the sticks, not some busy road in the centre of the city. Surely, it would be wrong of me to class it as a coincidence, wouldn't it?"

"I really don't know. What I do know is that you should make the DCI aware, or have you told her already?"

"No, I haven't mentioned it to her. All right, you win. I'll speak to her later." She glanced up at the clock on the wall. It was ten minutes to nine. The swing doors opened and Christine and Jill entered the room. "Morning, ladies, how are you both this morning?"

"Ready to hit the ground running," Christine replied.

"Ditto," Jill said, heading for the vending machine. "Is everything all right, boss?"

"Yes and no. I have some news that I'd rather share when the others are all here. I'll be in my office, give me a shout when they turn up."

Carla nodded and muttered under her breath, "An ideal time to ring the DCI."

"I wouldn't want to burden her with that type of info this early on in the day. I'll leave it until later, after I've shared my news with the team." She was about to move when the three remaining team members walked through the door. "Nice of you to join us, gentlemen. Grab yourself a coffee. I have some information I need to share with you all before we begin our day."

Will bought the coffees while the rest of the team moved their chairs into position.

"All set? Then I'll begin. Last night as I was leaving the station, the desk sergeant told me that a woman had been attacked in the heart of the city. Her attacker was riding, yes, you've guessed it, a moped. This is where the attack differs from the case we're already dealing with, in that the woman had acid thrown in her face."

"What? That's appalling," Carla said through gritted teeth.

"Indeed it is. I visited the woman in A&E last night. To say she was shocked by the events would be a gross understatement. The effects weren't pretty, take my word for that."

"How did it happen?" Barry asked, sitting forward in his chair, his elbows resting on his thighs.

"She'd just left work with a group of her colleagues. She was lagging behind the rest of the group because she was the one responsible for locking up the office. That's when her attacker struck. At first, she thought the person had thrown water in her face—that was until the burning started. She soon realised what had happened and screamed at her friends to help her. Those who had bottled water with them poured it over her face. Their swift reaction probably prevented the acid from doing more damage than was intended. As you can imagine, the poor woman is beside herself. Whether this is linked to the Wisdom case, well, that's what we need to investigate. My gut is telling me it is, so, I need you, Barry, to acquire another set of CCTV footage. Let's try and find something we can sink our teeth into."

"I'll get on it right away, boss. I'll need to know the address and roughly the time the incident occurred."

"Just after five-thirty on Broad Street. Quick as you can, Barry."

He manoeuvred his chair and immediately picked up his phone to request the footage from the control centre.

"While Barry's dealing with that, I want you guys to continue with the Wisdom case. Carla, can you chase up any possible sightings of the girl? I'm worried it's all gone quiet too soon. The response from the public so far has been very disappointing. I had anticipated and hoped it would have been better."

"I'll make some phone calls; it's not right that it's gone quiet. I'm with you on that one, boss."

"Okay, team. Let's get on with it. I'll be in my office should you need me. Barry, when you get to the attack on the footage, give me a shout right away."

"You've got it, boss. It shouldn't take me too long to find it."

"Good." She left the incident room and closed the door to her office, her heart beats increased as she walked around the desk, aware of what she needed to do next. She gulped down the moisture that had filled her mouth and dialled the number. "Hi, boss, I appreciate it's early, but do you have a second for a chat?"

"Sounds serious. Over the phone or in my office? I can spare you five minutes before my conference call is scheduled."

"That's all I need, over the phone is fine. Umm…I should have told you something a few months ago but I thought better of it."

"Skirting around the issue now isn't going to help matters, Inspector. Out with it." The DCI's voice was calm.

Sara couldn't help wondering how long that would last. "Well, you're aware that my cat was poisoned. What I neglected to tell you was that I received a threatening text not long after the last case was solved."

"Are you telling me the threat came from the suspect you arrested?"

"No. What I'm saying is that I thought the suspect I was chasing was behind the poisoning incident. The text came after he was in custody. There was no way he could have sent it to me."

"So who did, and why am I only hearing about this now?"

Sara sighed. "I guess I felt an idiot at the time. I genuinely thought he was behind it. When the text arrived it kind of floored me."

"What did the text say?"

There was no need for Sara to check her phone, the message was imprinted in her mind.

"'Your cat was lucky. It was a warning. Next time it'll be you who needs hospitalisation!'"

"Seriously? And you're only mentioning this now?" the DCI repeated, her voice high-pitched. "I don't have to tell you how angry I am about this, Inspector. Any time one of my officers is threatened like this I need to know immediately, you hear me?"

"I'm sorry, boss, it will never happen again, I swear."

"Glad to hear it. Now, what are you proposing we do about this?"

"Wait, I haven't finished." She went on to tell the chief what had taken place overnight with Mark's car. There was silence on the other end of the line for a few seconds. "DCI Price, are you still there?"

"I'm here. I'm digesting the information. Glad you're seeing someone at last. You shouldn't be alone, no one should. However, that type of behaviour is unnecessary and has to be stopped."

"I agree, but how do I go about putting a halt to it when I haven't got a clue who carried out the vandalism in the first place?"

"Hmm…it's a mess, that's what it is. Let me think it over and get back to you. Sorry to cut this conversation short, but my phone is lighting up. The people I have a conference call with are waiting."

"You go, I just wanted to make you aware, boss. I wouldn't lose any sleep over it."

"I won't, but I bet you will. We'll chat later on today."

Sara hung up as Barry poked his head round the door. "I've got the attack lined up, boss, if you want to take a peek." She slid her chair back and followed him out of the room.

Sara looked over Barry's shoulder as he played the footage. Knowing what to expect, she wanted to watch through her fingers but decided against it. "Hold it there, Barry. Team, gather around, we should all see this."

Barry pressed Play once the rest of the team were in place. There were a few gasps and 'ouches' thrown into the mix when they observed Angela being targeted by the thug.

"Bloody hell. What a bastard!" Carla said, voicing what everyone else was probably thinking.

"Barry, can you bring up the footage from the other day, the Wisdom incident? Let's see if we can see any similarities in the bike or the attacker that will give us an indication whether we're dealing with the same culprit or not."

Barry nodded and worked his magic. He had two monitors set up on his desk, each incident on a different screen. He ran the two footages simultaneously. Sara watched both, flicking her gaze between the monitors just like the rest of her team. "Damn, they're not the same," she stated, turning away from the screens in disgust.

Barry hit a button and paused both images. "Definitely different suspects. The one who attacked Angela is broader and is wearing a differently coloured helmet."

"I don't know much about helmets, but would it be worth checking out the local retailers? They both seem pretty distinctive designs to me."

"I can look into that, boss. A friend of mine has a bike shop in town," Craig volunteered.

"Does he now? You might want to check if he's sold any mopeds lately while you're at it, Craig."

"Okey doke."

"Right, let's get cracking, team. Report back to me with any news. I'll be in my den in the meantime." Sara nodded at the team and went back into her office, pausing briefly at the window to take in the magnificent view of the snow-capped Brecon Beacons in the distance.

So far, they had been lucky—they'd escaped the snow. She hoped that didn't change anytime soon. Last spring had been an absolute nightmare, around the time she had moved into her new home. When people had least expected it, many of them had been caught out and found themselves snowed in for a few days. The sudden drop in temperatures meant a lot of the roads became hazardous in the severe conditions. In the UK, they just weren't used to civilisation grinding to a halt. Sighing at recalling the fun times she had shared in the snow as a kid with her brother and sister made her suddenly miss them.

She hadn't rung either one of them in weeks, a month or so in her brother's case. Since Philip's death, they had both seemed distant, unsure how to act in her presence, which was nonsense, they were family. She made a mental note to ring them both at the weekend. *Here you go again, always putting off what you could do today!* She sat behind her desk to deal with the post, placing it into piles of urgency. Sara was caught up in the daily grind when Jill knocked on the door and eased it open.

"Come in, Jill. What's the frown of concern for?"

"I've been digging into any possible overnight sightings of Siobhan, boss."

"And? I'm thinking you've found something, am I right?"

Jill nodded and approached the desk. She handed Sara a sheet of paper. "I've printed off the report."

"Can you summarise it for me?"

Jill gulped and let out a large breath before she began, "Basically, the control centre received a call from a concerned man and woman. They were out driving in Gloucester and thought they saw a man with a child who looked very similar to Siobhan."

"In Gloucester. Has someone chased it up?"

"Yes, a uniformed officer went to see the couple and took down their statement. The man tried to speak with the guy with the child but received a punch in the face for his efforts. The guy then fled with the girl."

"Crap, sounds like them, yes?"

"I'm thinking along those lines, but Gloucester! Should we widen the search, perhaps?"

"I'd say so. Get on to the main station in Gloucester, make them aware of the situation and ask them to keep an eye open for us."

"Will do."

"Do you know if Craig has had any luck yet?"

"I think he rang his friend but he was out at the time, he's due back soon."

"Okay, thanks. I'll be out when I've finished this laborious task."

Jill smiled and left the room. Sara sighed heavily once the door was shut again, her frustration rising at their lack of information on Siobhan.

At least the man had tried to save the little girl, which is more than some folks manage nowadays. It takes balls to approach someone you suspect of abducting a child. That person could pull a knife at the drop of a hat. Damn, what the hell are Siobhan and the other missing children going through? Are the moped cases linked?

Although there was an underlying doubt running through her mind, the answer still remained a certainty—they had to be linked.

Why? Why now? Maybe the attacks would be a thing of the past now that every officer on duty was on the lookout for possible suspects. She'd given the order to stop and search if need be. Those instructions should mean the people of Hereford were safe once more, shouldn't they? Only time would tell on that one.

She rang the hospital to check how Angela Guppy was. The ward sister on duty told her the woman had a comfortable night but was understandably feeling down. There was nothing Sara could do about that except capture the person responsible. She turned her attention to her paperwork, which took longer than anticipated to go through, mainly because she found herself distracted by the what-ifs surrounding the case, the kind she hated running through her mind. Sara was one of those people who preferred to deal with facts not *possible* facts. She left her office a couple of hours later and visited each of the team members to see what they'd discovered in her absence, which sadly turned out to be not much.

"Craig, any news on your helmet friend?"

"He got back to me a little while ago, boss. I sent him the images of the helmets. He told me that he'd sold two very similar in the past few weeks."

"Okay, I'm liking the way this is heading. Why aren't you smiling?"

His right shoulder hitched up. "Because when he looked through his records, he came to the conclusion the persons paid cash."

"Damn, so no paper trail for us to follow," Sara said, filling in the gap.

"Exactly."

"Has he sold any mopeds lately? Don't tell me they were all paid for in cash, too?"

"No. He said he hadn't sold any mopeds, not for at least six months or so, said people rarely bought them nowadays. The last one was to a woman."

"In your opinion, what's the likelihood of either of those suspects being a woman?"

He shook his head. "Not likely, boss. The frame is too broad to be a woman. She'd need to be down the gym seven days a week to get a physique like that."

"Voice of experience talking?" she asked, examining his physique for the first time.

"I've been known to lift weights. I visit the gym when time permits, at least three times a week. I'd have to work a lot harder to match those two guys."

"Might be worth speaking to the local gyms in the area then, yes?"

"I had the same idea. I've contacted three of them so far. They're dubious about giving information out over the phone."

"Legwork it is then. Why don't you take Will with you?" Sara glanced over at the older man who nodded his approval. "You know the type of things to ask. If you can get an address, that'll be good. Search the car park at the gyms for a moped while you're there."

Craig and Will left the incident room just as the phone on Carla's desk rang. "Boss, it's Jeff for you."

Sara smiled and took the phone from her partner. "Hi, Jeff, what can I do for you?"

"I have a young man in reception wanting to see you, boss," he said, a certain amount of mischief in his tone.

"A young man, eh? Is he tall, dark-haired and handsome?"

"He is indeed. Says he wants to see you, only if you have the time, though."

"I'll be down in a jiffy." She hung up and stepped into her office, she checked out her appearance in the small mirror in her handbag and ran a comb through her hair then left her office again.

"No, is this your new fella?" Carla asked, pushing her chair back and getting to her feet.

Sara pointed at her. "It might be. Shame you're busy, otherwise I'd introduce you."

Carla flopped into her chair again and pouted. "I only wanted a quick introduction, nothing fancy."

"You'll get it, eventually, just not now. He's here on important business, remember."

A smile replaced her partner's pout. "Okay, consider my wrist slapped. Maybe we could go on a double date one day."

Sara laughed. "Or maybe not," she called over her shoulder as she headed for the door.

She entered the reception area to find Mark talking to the desk sergeant. He surprised her by placing a gentle kiss on her lips. Her cheeks flared up when she caught Jeff smirking.

"Hi, any news on getting your car repaired?"

"I dropped it off at my mate's garage. I know it was probably the wrong thing to do when making a complaint. I've taken photos though. My friend has loaned me a car, thank goodness, so I can still go on my course in a few days."

"The pictures should suffice. That's excellent news. Did he think the cause was paint stripper?"

"Yep, he told me he hadn't seen anything like it in over twenty years. Lucky me, eh?"

She rubbed his arm. "Sorry it happened to you, Mark, you didn't deserve this shit."

"Does anyone?"

"True enough. Have you finished your statement?"

"We've only just started, boss. I can get on with something else if you two want a chat," Jeff responded.

"I wish I had the time. We're up to our necks in it up there at the moment." She pulled Mark away from the desk and over to the corner. "Look, there's something you should know."

"I'm not going to like this, am I?" Mark replied, frowning.

"I need to say it. Maybe it's my suspicious mind working overtime, but perhaps we should call it a day between us."

"What? Are you kidding? Over a little spilt paint stripper? I can't see why you'd want to let that deter you. Shit happens, right?"

She glanced over her shoulder at Jeff. She knew he was only pretending to be busy and listening to their conversation. She took hold of Mark's arm and steered him outside the station. It wasn't long before she regretted her decision, only dressed in a suit. She shuddered against the cold. "All I'm saying is, and not making a good job of it so far, you know as well as I do what happened to Misty. It seems to me that I'm being targeted." *Do I tell him about the message I was sent or not?*

He shook his head. "All right, I agree that Misty was deliberately poisoned, but surely if someone had it in for you, why pick on my car instead of yours? And why wait until now to strike? We've been seeing each other for over a month now."

She leant in and lowered her voice. "That was the first time you'd stayed over. All right, the person who vandalised your car couldn't have known that you spent the night on the couch..."

He paced the paved area outside the main entrance and ran a hand through his hair. "Bollocks, that's true. Christ, what a predicament to be in." He looked down at the ground and shuffled his feet, worry lines appearing on his face.

"That's why I think we should call it a day," she repeated, her breath catching in her throat.

He shocked her when he gripped both of her arms. "Is that what you truly want, Sara? I thought we were getting along just fine."

"We were, I mean we *are*. I'm not saying this lightly, Mark. I'm suggesting it to protect you. There are things that have gone on in my past that you don't know about."

"What? Are you telling me you're a serial killer and only pretending to be a police officer?"

She rolled her head back and laughed. "No, I'm not saying that at all. I'm a genuine police officer and devoted to my job. There are certain aspects of it that can be detrimental to my personal life, though."

"I know sometimes you're guilty of taking work home with you, aren't we all? I'm forced to do the same at times, but we can overcome these things, Sara. Unless, of course, you're seeing this as a get-out clause. You've tried to finish it with me before but haven't had the guts to do it? Is that it? The perfect excuse has arisen, and you're running for the hills rather than face the demons, your demons? I haven't pushed you, have I?"

"No, that's not the case at all. I really like you. I'm saying all this because I'm trying to *protect* you from getting hurt."

His grip tightened. "I'm willing to take my chances if you are?"

She tried to dislodge herself from his arms, but his grip tightened even more, not in a menacing kind of way, in a way that told her how desperate he was for them to continue what they had. Her eyes pricked. His expression had turned into one of desperation.

"All right. I'm willing to forge ahead, if that's what you truly want?"

"It is. Without sounding too needy, I think we've made a vital connection at last. It might have taken a few weeks for you to relax in my presence, but we're there now. Why let some idiot ruin our chance of happiness? Gosh, did that sound too mushy? Enough to frighten you off maybe?"

Sara smiled. His hands left her arms.

"No, not too mushy. I really like you, Mark, but if the time ever arises that you want to call a halt to things, promise me you'll do it. Not everyone can stand being a copper's partner."

He held up his little finger for her to shake. "Pinky promise. I think we've been making great strides in recent weeks. I'm happy how things have progressed between us, even if you did make me sleep on the couch last night."

She bit her lip. "Sorry. I'm not ready for anything else, not yet."

"I understand that. We continue with the promise that I will never force you to do anything you're not ready to do, okay?"

"Okay. You're a special man, Mark. I knew that already, but what's happened over the last twelve hours has reinforced that. When you saw the state of your car, you could have exploded. I think most men would have, given the choice. That told me a lot about you. Do you mind if we go inside now? I'm bloody freezing."

He smiled. "On one proviso."

"Name it."

"That you give me a kiss."

She leant forward, placed a hand on either side of his face and shared a kiss. Something inside her stirred. She sensed someone looking at them through the door and opened her eyes to find Carla standing there, her arms folded, a smug grin on her face. Sara pulled away from Mark and wiped a hand across her lips.

"Sorry, I better get back to work. As much as you're a welcome distraction, if the chief caught me skiving, she'd demote me by the end of the week." Which was a total fabrication on her part, but it sounded a good enough excuse to get back to work and inside out of the cold.

"That's a shame. I was enjoying that. Do you want me to drop by this evening?"

"You can if you want. Give me a ring later. I'd hate to make arrangements and have to postpone at the last minute. The rate this week is going, I don't suppose I'll be home at my normal time."

"I'll do that. Thanks for popping down to see me. It was definitely worth the visit." He licked his lips.

When they returned to the reception area, Carla was nowhere in sight.

"I'll leave you in Jeff's capable hands. Speak later, Mark."

"Count on it." He smiled and returned his attention to the desk sergeant.

Sara rushed up the stairs and barged through the doors to the incident room. Carla was sitting at her desk, pretending to search for something on her computer.

Sara walked up behind her and bent down to whisper in her ear. "I didn't have you pegged as a voyeur. Do you get off on spying on people?" She walked towards the vending machine and asked if anyone wanted a drink. When she glanced Carla's way, the colour had risen in her cheeks.

She handed around the drinks and went back into her office. Two seconds later, Carla stepped into the room, her head bowed.

"Did you want something, partner?"

"Only to apologise. I didn't mean to make you feel uncomfortable. I was intrigued. It's obvious how much this guy means to you."

"It is? I hadn't realised that. You're forgiven. Don't push things, though, Carla. It's taken me months to confide in you about what's gone on in my past. Don't make me regret my decision."

"Can I make up for my mistake by taking you to lunch?"

"There's no need for that. A sandwich will suffice. A steak and prawn one I fancy with lashings of chips on the side. That should set you back twenty quid."

Carla's mouth dropped open.

"Get outta here, I'm winding you up. A tuna mayo sandwich on brown will do."

"Phew, I thought I was going to have to apply for a second mortgage for a moment there." They both laughed. "In all seriousness, he seems a nice chap, really good-looking."

"Did you think I'd be unable to hook a man so handsome, is that what you're saying?"

Carla cringed. "Crap! Why don't I keep my mouth shut from now on?"

"Hooray, I'd welcome that." Sara applauded.

"You can be nasty at times, you know that? I've apologised until I'm blue in the face, and it still isn't good enough, is it?"

"I accepted your apology. There's no harm in making you suffer for the grief you've given me, though."

"Can we call a truce?"

"Fine by me. I'm starving. I could do with that sandwich now."

"Love has that effect on you," Carla mumbled when she turned and left the room.

"I heard that, you cheeky mare." Once she was alone again, she wondered if Carla was onto something. Was she guilty of opening up her heart to Mark?

CHAPTER 6

THE AFTERNOON FLEW PAST. Craig and Will reported back that they'd failed to find anything out at the gyms, and that put them back at first base again. The team were getting ready to pack up for the evening when Carla accepted a call. Sara was standing at the whiteboard, going over the case details when Carla clicked her fingers to gain her attention.

"The boss is here, Jeff, I'm going to put you on speaker, so we can all hear what you have to say." Carla pressed a button on the phone.

"Jeff, what's up?" Sara asked, walking towards Carla's desk.

"Reports are coming in, ma'am, that there's been another incident involving a moped in the city again."

"What happened, Jeff?"

"A woman was killed, boss."

"Carla, grab your coat. We'll be down in a sec. Have the details handy for me. Give Barry the location. He can start trawling through the CCTV footage."

She dipped into the office to collect her coat and handbag and tapped Carla on the shoulder as she passed. "Get a wriggle on. Time's not on our side at this hour of the day."

They raced down the stairs. Sara held out her hand when she reached the reception desk.

"Good luck, boss. I've instructed the patrol cars in the area to be on the lookout."

"Great work, thanks, Jeff."

Sara pressed the key fob and dropped into her seat. "You better get the light on. I have a feeling we're going to need to use the siren on this one."

Carla plonked the light on top of the car and placed her hand on the switch ready to engage the siren once they hit traffic. "Bloody hell. This week is going from bad to worse. Maybe it would be better if we swapped our shifts. The incidents all seem to be happening around the same time."

Sara nodded. "You could be onto something there. Once we've attended the scene, I'll get you to inform the team. We could do eleven to nine, just until these crimes are solved."

"I'm sure the rest of the team would be up for that."

"Great, that's settled then. We'll begin tomorrow. Bye-bye social life for a few weeks."

"Your man won't be too happy about that."

"I can't help that. Solving this case is paramount for me."

"Your dedication might cause a rift between you," Carla suggested cautiously.

"If it does, then so be it." *I'd hate for that to happen, but if it comes down to it, at this moment in time the job will always win. It's seen me through the darkest period of my life. I'd feel shitty if I turned my back on it now. Men will come and go like the breeze, Mum told me when I'd first started dating. Maybe she's right about that. Although I'd kind of like to hang on to the one I've got for now.*

The traffic was horrendous in parts, especially around the city centre. "Remind me why I rarely drive through this part of town at this time of night again?"

"I'm the same. It's a pain in the rear."

"The sooner they get that bypass up and running, the better. Even if it is to the detriment of the residents in the projected area. This city's roads need improving, and quickly."

"On one hand I agree, on the other, my aunt lives in the area they're proposing to build the bypass. I feel for her. She can't sell up at the drop of a hat. Who will want to buy her quaint cottage now that the plans are going through?"

"That's a shame. Sorry, Carla, I had no idea. All right, I've had enough, flick the damn switch."

The siren sounded. They were bumper to bumper in one of the three lanes; there was no getting out of the situation until the lights changed. Sara drummed her fingers on the steering wheel, and once the traffic started moving again, eased herself into the outer lane and put her foot down.

They arrived at the scene a few minutes later. Lorraine's dyed bright-red hair stuck out like a sore thumb in the crowd of people surrounding the body. "Shit! There are too many around here. We need to get them cleared ASAP. Can you do that while I speak to Lorraine?"

"Idiots. I'm on it. I'll get the cordon extended." Carla trotted ahead and, using her arms, helped to guide the onlookers back. She had a word with a couple of the uniformed officers already at the scene. Once Carla had successfully moved the pedestrians back, the two officers adjusted the tape to a new position, to where it should have been in the first place.

Relieved, Sara approached Lorraine who was in the process of pulling on a white paper suit. "Hi, I take it you've only just arrived."

"Yep, I'd stand well clear if I were you. I'm pretty pissed off with your lot. Whatever possessed them to place the tape there? This area should be clear of this mob. My guys are going to have to erect a marquee now."

Sara nodded her understanding. "Come on, you'd have to put a tent up anyway, don't go blaming uniform."

"All right. Maybe I'm just pissed off because I thought I was going to finish at a reasonable time for a change and had plans."

"And you thought you were going to get laid tonight, right?"

"That might be close to the truth. I've had my eye on this bloke for months." She kicked out at a nearby stone.

"All right, calm down, you nearly put that through the shop window and that stone could be evidence."

"Oops. I'm calm. Right, let's see what we've got. You being here, I'm presuming you think this case is related to the one we attended the other day, involving the train. What was the victim's name again?" She raised her hand to stop Sara from filling in the details. "It's coming...Wisdom, wasn't it? I've had an influx of PMs this week. One case tends to go into the next until I've had time to sort out the paperwork. I apologise now if you haven't heard from me regarding the case."

"I have. Stop stressing."

"I thrive on stress ordinarily, you know that. But getting laid is something that only comes around once in a blue moon."

"I know how that feels," Sara agreed.

"Ha! You could get laid every day of the week, a pretty wench like you. Me, a dried-up old prune, has to grab her chances when they come along, which isn't that often the more wrinkles that come my way."

"Jesus, you talk a lot of shit at times, Lorraine. What are you? Thirty-nine, forty?"

"The latter. It's all downhill for me now. Hang on to your youth while you've got the chance, that's my advice on the matter."

"What a lot of bullshit spews out of your mouth."

"It's a fact. Enough about my dour, non-existent love life, let's see what this doll has to say about her death."

Sara took her own set of white overalls from the boot of Lorraine's van and togged up. Together they approached the body. There was evidence that the woman had been run over—a tyre mark on her crushed face and down the length of her cream overcoat. She searched the area and spotted a man and woman comforting each other. "I'll be right back."

"Charming," Lorraine muttered.

The man and woman appeared devastated. "Hello, I'm DI Sara Ramsey. Am I right in thinking that you witnessed what happened?"

The man hugged the woman. "Yes, my wife and I had just left one of the shops. It was awful. I tried to help her but before I realised what was going on it was too late. The bus hit her...ran over her," the man corrected himself.

"I'm so sorry you had to witness the accident. Are you up to speaking to me? I quite understand if you'd prefer to leave it a day or two. It's just that the sooner we can get to the truth, the better chance we have of tracking down the person responsible."

"No, I want to tell you. They say talking about things like this makes the situation better, don't they?"

"That's supposed to happen, yes."

"Like I said, my wife and I left one of the shops. We were having a conversation when I heard a noise behind us. There was a damn moped on the pavement, heading our way. I shoved Laura aside and tried to tackle the driver. I missed. The guy carried on down the pavement and started circling around the woman, the woman who was killed. Laura begged me not to get involved, but I had to. I ran to help the woman, but by the time I got there, well, it was too late. The guy on the moped managed to wrestle the woman's handbag out of her arm. He then jabbed his bike at her, as if he was threatening to drive at her. She started backing up. I tried to tell her to watch out, but it was too late. The guy forced her to back up so much that she lost her footing and fell off the pavement. The bus driver couldn't have avoided her. He must be devastated. He's over there; he'll be able to corroborate his part in the accident."

"What did the driver do then, of the moped, I mean?"

"He paused for the briefest of moments, revved his bike then took off. We were both gobsmacked. I was the one who called it in."

"Thank you for doing what you did. Do you want us to take your statement now, so you can go home?"

"If you wouldn't mind. I think my wife is in shock. I need to get her home in the warm." The man rubbed his hands up and down his wife's arms.

She rested her head on his chest, and fresh tears fell onto her cheeks.

"I'll get that sorted now." Sara smiled and crossed the pavement to the pedestrian area where Carla was chatting to one of the officers. "Carla, do me a favour and get a couple of statements down. The couple standing over there witnessed the incident. They want to get home in the warm but want to do the statement before they go."

Carla turned to the officer. "Have you got any statement forms in your car?"

The man nodded and rushed over to his vehicle parked a few feet away. He returned with four or five forms and handed them to Carla.

"Thanks." Sara walked back with Carla and introduced her to the couple then continued on her journey to where Lorraine and her team were standing. "I've got the lowdown on what happened if you want to hear it?"

"Let's get inside the tent first."

A SOCO team member raised his thumb, giving them the go-ahead to enter the quickly erected marquee.

Sara ran through what the witness had told her. "That sums it up."

"Downright disgusting. Maybe if the moped fiend hadn't forced her to step backwards we would be calling this a bloody robbery gone wrong, but not now, surely."

"I agree. It was a deliberate act. I intend to punish this man with everything I can throw at him, if we ever catch the bastard."

"Think positively. It's obvious this person has an agenda. Are they random acts or have his victims been specifically targeted?" Lorraine said.

"That's the sixty-four-million-dollar question that I intend to get the answer to. I have my guys back at the station looking over the footage. Hopefully something significant will come from that. You won't be aware of this, but last night I was called out to an acid attack on a young woman. She's still in hospital."

"Crap! Don't tell me someone threw it in her face?"

"Yep. Sick fuckers. That's her ruined for life now. There's a limit to what a plastic surgeon will be able to do to repair the damage. All she was guilty of was walking home after work, minding her own business. I've always regarded this place as a safe city to live in, well, since I arrived nearly two years ago."

Lorraine wagged her finger. "Now don't go taking this personally, that's a coincidence."

"Is it, though? Who can tell? Philip was gunned down in broad daylight; I was there moments after it happened. What if the perps saw me and are targeting me? I have a new fella, and his car was vandalised last night. It was sitting outside my house. My cat was also hurt a few months back."

"Now you're being paranoid. You can't think along those lines." Lorraine nudged her. "Glad you're getting some action at last, on the dating front."

"I'm not, that's just it. Mark stayed the night on the couch. I'm not ready to take our relationship to the next level. Anyway, I digress. I'm bound to take stock of everything going on in my life and make assumptions, aren't I?"

"Assumptions that aren't factual are a dangerous game to get involved in, Sara. My advice would be not to muddy the water. Work with what you've got for now. A possible link might show up in the future."

"Thanks, I needed that. Can you get me some form of ID? I better inform the next of kin before it appears on the news."

"I'll do my best. I haven't seen any handbag lying around."

"Damn, the witness told me the driver stole her handbag. Maybe she has a phone in her pocket, that's where I keep mine most of the time."

Lorraine crouched and searched the woman's coat pocket. "Ah, we're in luck, it's intact."

"That's great, all we need now is to get into it."

"If you have a problem, my tech guys can probably help crack that."

Sara exhaled a frustrated breath. "That's going to take time."

"What's the alternative?"

"There isn't one. Okay, I'll leave it with you. Why did the woman have to be alone?"

"Your best option is if someone reports her missing," Lorraine replied, giving her some hope to hang on to.

"Okay, I'll leave this with you then and get back to the station. Thanks, Lorraine, send your report through when you can."

"Will do. Good luck finding an ID for the woman. I'll get my guys working on the phone ASAP."

Sara smiled and left the tent. Carla was still in the process of taking down the statements. Sara strode around the area, trying to suss out where the accident had actually taken place. Since the body had been moved out of the road to allow the traffic to flow again. A man wearing a peaked cap approached her.

"This is the spot. I couldn't avoid her."

Sara turned to see tears glistening in the man's eyes. She rubbed his arm to comfort him. "I'm sorry you had to go through this. It must be hard for you right now."

"It is. I gave my statement ages ago and should be out of here by now. I can't leave. Knowing that I killed that woman is keeping me glued to the spot."

"It wasn't your fault. I've heard how it went down; you couldn't have avoided her. Were you speeding?"

"Definitely not."

"Then you're not to blame. Things will look brighter in the morning. I know that's hard to accept right now, but please, don't take this on your shoulders. It was an accident, pure and simple."

"Unlike any accident I've ever had. I'm gutted. Feel sick to my stomach. I rang my boss. First thing he asked me was just that, was I speeding? You know what his second question was?"

Sara shook her head.

"Was I drunk? What the fuck is that all about? The woman stepped off the pavement into my path. It's three lanes around here; there's no way I could have avoided hitting her. If I'd changed lanes there's a possibility I might have killed someone else, for fuck's sake. Have you ever tried manoeuvring one of those things at the click of your fingers? It's an impossible task I tell you, bloody impossible. Now I'm going to have this on my conscience for the rest of my working life and beyond."

"It's going to be hard for you to move on from this, I know, but you're going to have to do it, otherwise your life could spiral out of control. It wasn't your fault. You have to keep telling yourself that over and over if you have to. Does your company have a counsellor on hand you can visit?"

"Do they heck. In any case, I ain't gonna see no shrink."

"It's not a shrink. It's someone you can speak honestly and openly with. Believe me, it'll help you get your working life back on track. If you don't…well, that doesn't bear thinking about, does it?"

"Agreed. All right. You've persuaded me. Are you the officer in charge of the case?"

"Yes."

"Catch the bastard who was terrorising the woman before her death. I saw what he did to her, it was shocking. He deserves to hang for what he did."

"I sometimes wish they'd bring back hanging for certain crimes. I guess some people regard it as barbaric and are glad that we no longer live in the past."

"Ha! Barbaric my arse. What that little shit did was barbaric, and he should be held accountable."

"I'm going to do my very best to find him, I promise you that."

"Good luck. I'm going to head home now."

"Glad to hear it. Things like this happen all the time. There's no point dwelling on situations you can't alter."

The man nodded and went on his way. Carla joined her a few seconds later. "All done?" Sara asked.

"Yep. What a tragedy. Let's hope we can find the bastards soon."

"Why? Why are they targeting this area all of a sudden? Something must have triggered it, Carla."

"Until we find out what that trigger is, our hands are bloody tied."

"Agreed. Let's get back to the station and put our heads together."

"What about going to see the victim's family?"

"No can do right now. Her phone was on her, but it was locked.

Lorraine is going to get the tech guys on it and get back to me. The woman's handbag was stolen."

"Bummer."

"I'll leave a note on Maddy's desk in case a relative reports her missing in the meantime."

"Had we better take a pic of the victim? It may not be the perfect solution, but..."

"I suppose we should have something to compare her to if anyone comes forward."

Carla fished her phone out of her pocket. "I'll do it."

"Thanks. I need to make a call, then we'll set off." She watched Carla walk away and turned her back. "Hi, Mark. A quick update for you. I'm out and about investigating another murder. No idea when I'm likely to return home, sorry."

"That's too bad. Crap, your workload just got heavier by the sound of things."

"You're not wrong there. I've arranged to change my shift for the next week or so as well, so that means I won't likely see you until the weekend. Sorry to let you down."

"There's no need to apologise. I'm going away for a few days anyway, remember. We'll make up for it on Saturday night as planned. I've booked the table, so there's no turning back now."

"You have? Where?"

"Miller and Carter's Steakhouse. If you've never been there, it's fabulous."

"Sounds expensive."

"You're worth it. Ring me when time permits. I've got to go, I have my next patient waiting."

"Thanks for being so understanding. You're the best."

"Take care out there, Sara."

"Don't start worrying about me. I'm Taser-trained and I have an excellent team around me."

"Glad to hear it. Cheerio for now."

"Have fun on your course if I don't chat to you before you leave."

"Thanks."

Sara ended the call, sadness sweeping over her at the prospect of not seeing Mark for a few days. *It's only a few days, and I have a hot date to look forward to on Saturday. Providing nothing major crops up. Ha! Nothing major! Two murders, an abduction and an acid attack on the cards already. What else would constitute as being called 'major'?*

"Ready to go? You seemed miles away then. Anything wrong? Apart from the obvious, I mean."

"Nothing that can't be fixed. Let's go." The journey back was as congested as the one they'd experienced an hour before. "Give us a break, people, you should all be home enjoying your evening meals by now."

"There's a thought," Carla said. "Good job I knocked up a chilli at the weekend and froze it. I can defrost it when I get home later."

"Doesn't Andrew cook?"

"Now and again. He'd rather ring out for a takeaway than rattle around in the kitchen during the week. It's a different story at the weekend, though; we share the cooking then. I generally make a batch of meals we can pull from the freezer when something like this crops up."

"Bloody hell, you're organised," Sara said, admiring her partner's attempt at domesticity.

"I never used to be, not before Andrew showed up. I guess women alter their way of thinking when they have a man around to share their lives."

Sara relived what her own home life had consisted of when Philip had been around. Nothing similar to what Carla was suggesting. "No matter how much I loved Philip, I don't think I ever changed my routine for him. Yes, I cooked and cleaned, nothing more than that. If anything, we shared the chores around the house."

"He sounded an ideal partner. Any idea what's going to happen with you and this new fella?"

"Don't ask. I tried to warn him off me this afternoon when he dropped by the station."

"What? Are you *crazy*? Why would you do that?"

"To protect him."

"The warning text?"

Sara sighed. "If someone has a grudge against me personally, they have no right to include Mark. He doesn't deserve that. I'd rather be sat at home alone than include him in any trouble coming my way."

"I think you need to take a breath and not do anything rash that you'll probably regret later. If Mark is willing to keep seeing you, then what's the harm? And believe me, he seemed pretty willing to me from what I witnessed at the station earlier."

Sara grinned and swiped Carla's arm. "Okay, you've talked me round. Let's see how things pan out over the next week or so, and I'll go from there."

"Excellent idea. Although I'd lengthen that time frame to two weeks or even a month," Carla replied as Sara reversed into her parking space at the station.

"We'll see. Enough personal talk, back to the job in hand."

They entered the station.

"All right, Jeff?"

"Appears to be, apart from the call I passed on earlier, ma'am."

"All dealt with now. There was no ID on the victim. Can you let the control room know in case a relative calls to inform us she's missing?"

"I'll get on to it now."

"I should be around for the next few hours, so ring me if you hear anything."

"That I will."

When they reached the top of the stairs, DCI Price was standing there, briefcase in hand, looking as if she was about to leave for the evening. "Are you two coming back from somewhere?"

"Yes, ma'am. You go ahead, Carla, I'll fill the chief in." Sara watched her partner go through the swing doors of the incident room. "We've been at a murder scene for the past few hours, and yes, we think there's a connection to the other cases we're investigating as there was a moped involved."

"What happened? I better hear the whole story. Come on, we'll go into the incident room."

Sara nodded and led the way. The room was silent when they entered, the team busy with their individual tasks. DCI Price placed her briefcase on the floor beside her and crossed her arms, the sleeves of her grey woollen coat straining at the seams.

Sara explained how the incident had occurred, then turned to Barry. "Did you manage to obtain the footage, Barry?"

"Yes, boss. Do you want me to run it?"

"Do you want to see for yourself, boss?" Sara asked, unsure if the DCI's stomach would stand up to seeing the gruesome crime.

"Might as well as I'm here."

Once they were in position behind Barry's chair, Sara placed a hand on his shoulder. "Wait, is your computer linked to the TV screen? We can all view it at the same time."

"It is. Linking it now." Barry hit a button and switched on the TV with the remote control sitting on his desk.

The screen lit up, and the footage began. The victim and the witnesses Sara had spoken to, the man and his wife, could be seen in the distance. Sara searched the screen beyond them and pointed out the moped as it mounted the pavement and drove towards the victim.

"He's got some nerve, I'll give him that," DCI Price noted.

"It's sickening, his audacious behaviour, I mean."

They watched intently as the crime unfolded before them. At times, Sara viewed the images through narrowed eyes, aware of how the crime had happened and what had led up to the woman walking backwards into the path of the bus.

The DCI was pretty vocal as she viewed the incident, sharing plenty of gasps and 'ouches' along with the rest of the team until the victim's life ended. Everyone in the room fell silent for a few seconds until Sara told Barry to switch off the TV.

"That's what we're up against, boss."

"Okay, I'm kind of wishing I hadn't been privy to that. The image is bound to live with me for a while."

"Welcome to our world," Sara replied with a hint of a smile.

"The victim's name? Do we have that yet?"

"Nope. Hopefully the tech guys will be able to unlock her phone and give us some contact information soon."

"Unless she's single, either way I'm guessing her family will be worried sick about her if she fails to show up this evening."

"I've asked the desk sergeant to inform the control room. He'll let me know if any such calls come in over the course of the next few hours. I have something to tell you...we've decided to alter our shifts around a little. The reason being that all these crimes appear to be happening about the time we're due to end our shift."

"What did you have in mind, Inspector?"

"Starting around eleven and working until nine. Would that be all right with you?"

DCI Price scratched the side of her face. "I don't like the idea of the incident room being unmanned first thing in the morning. You have enough staff here, let one of them continue their normal shift pattern, that way the phones are covered."

"Okay, you're right. We'll draw straws."

DCI Price swivelled and returned to her briefcase. She picked it up and headed for the door. "Keep me informed regularly on this one. Enjoy the rest of your evening, team." She left the room before anyone could respond.

"Sorry, everyone, I should've rung you to check if you were up to swapping shifts," Carla announced.

All of them muttered their response and nodded, except one person, Jill Smalling.

"Is there a problem, Jill?" Sara asked, noting her reluctance.

"There might be. It's a little personal, boss. All right if I speak to you in your office?"

"Of course. Come through. Let's crack on for the next thirty minutes or so, team, then call it a night."

Jill followed Sara into her office.

Once they were both seated, Sara asked, "What's troubling you?"

"Not sure where to begin really."

Sara smiled to put the sergeant at ease. "At the beginning is always useful. You seem worried."

"I am. It's called having two teenage girls. My dilemma is that Wayne's away a lot of the time, so the childcare is generally down to me."

"Wayne's a lorry driver if I remember rightly."

"That's correct, boss. Well, when I'm at work, doing my usual shift, Mum helps me out. She scoots over to my house about three-thirty, which means she's there when the girls come home from school. The thing is, she generally leaves the second I step through the door. I really don't want to screw up her routine. Our relationship recently has turned a little fractious. I'm worried if I mess her around swapping my shift, she'll tell me to do one and I'd be forced to get someone else to look after the kids. On my wage that's gonna be difficult to cover. We're stretched to the limits with our bills as it is."

Sara raised her hand. "You're making more of a problem of this than is necessary. As the chief suggested, we should have one person stick to their usual shift—that person is you. Problem solved, right?"

Jill let out the breath she'd been holding in. "Thank you. You've just saved me ten years of grief, boss."

"Okay, for a start, I don't ever want you to feel awkward coming to me with a personal problem, got that?" Jill nodded. "And secondly, my philosophy remains the same: happy staff makes for a happy environment. If anyone on this team has issues, they need to run them past me. There's no need to dwell on a matter if it can be easily rectified. We're all going to have personal issues to deal with now and again. It's called life. I should know. The past two years have torn me apart, but I'm on the mend now. Do you know why that is, Jill?"

"Because you've gone through the grieving process now?"

"There's that, but also because I have you guys around me. You're an ace team, we're an ace team. We watch each other's back and come up with a solution to ensure peace and harmony are maintained. Crap, that sounded flowery even for me, but you get my drift."

Jill chuckled. "You're one in a million, boss. So glad you transferred down here a few years ago. It has been a pleasure working alongside you. You're pretty special considering the heartbreak you've suffered recently. Gosh, that's me being all mushy now."

Sara sniggered. "Touché. So that's you sorted then. You'll continue to man the phones et cetera until we all arrive at eleven. You'll only be alone for two hours."

"That'll soon fly. Thanks for understanding my predicament, boss. I'd think again about having kids if I had my time over. Ouch! I can't believe I said that. Makes me out to be a bad mother. I'm not, honestly. What I was getting at is that I love my job and sometimes I feel bad when my personal life interferes with what goes on here."

"There you go again, being too harsh on yourself. We needed someone to man the phones. That responsibility could have fallen on anyone's shoulders, but it fell on yours. Job done. Now get out of here. I'll see you in the morning."

"Thanks, boss." Jill left the room.

Sara sighed. She was lucky she was surrounded by good people. She couldn't help wondering how different her transition might have been if she'd had a different team around her.

After a few minutes' reflection, she rejoined the team.

Carla was on the phone and looked her way. "Thanks for that, we'll chase it up right away."

Sara tilted her head. "What's that?"

"SOCO. They've given me the woman's home phone number—it was indicated as that on her mobile anyway."

"Okay, I'll make the call." Sara dialled the number.

A man answered within a few rings. "Hello."

"Hello, sir, you don't know me. I'm DI Sara Ramsey of the West Mercia Police."

"Okay, why are you ringing me?" He gasped as if it had just dawned on him. "No, it's not to do with Tina, is it?"

"Is Tina your wife, sir?"

"Yes. I was expecting her home about an hour ago."

"Have you tried contacting your wife, sir?"

"No. I came home myself a couple of hours ago and have been looking after my three-year-old daughter ever since. Why are you ringing me? Has something happened to my wife?"

"Maybe it would be better if I came to see you, sir."

"Okay, now I'm worried."

"Your address?" Sara was determined not to share any bad news over the phone, it wasn't her style.

"Sixteen Edgar Road, Tupsley."

"Okay, I'll be there within the next fifteen minutes. Try not to worry."

"That's easy for you to say. My gut is telling me a different story. I'll see you then."

Sara hung up and exhaled a deep breath. "Shit, what a great way to end a shift. All right, gang. Let's call it a day. I was hoping I'd be able to tell the relatives before the day was over. Carla, you can either leave this with me or tag along for the ride."

"I don't mind coming with you for moral support. I'll take my car and go directly home from there, if that's all right with you?"

"Of course it is."

CHAPTER 7

SARA LEFT her car and waited for Carla to lock her vehicle before they both approached the mid-terraced house together. A few kids were riding bikes up and down in the quiet street even though dark had set in a few hours earlier.

Sara rang the bell. The door was immediately opened by a man in his early thirties, his hair messed up as though he'd been raking his fingers through it during the wait. She flashed her ID and introduced Carla.

The man stepped back to allow them access. "We'll go through to the kitchen. My daughter, Emily, is distracted with her toys. She shouldn't bother us. I'm Brian, by the way."

They entered the large kitchen to find a happy toddler sitting on a blanket on the tiled floor, playing with a set of dolls. Sara motioned for Carla to play with the girl while she spoke to the father. In the hallway, she'd noticed a family picture, and her heart skipped several beats. There was no doubting that Tina was the victim who'd stepped into the bus's path.

"I know it's bad news. How bad is it?" Brian asked, keeping his voice low to avoid upsetting his daughter.

Sara followed his lead. She leant in and broke the news. "I'm sorry.

Earlier on this evening, your wife was involved in an incident. I'm sorry to tell you that she lost her life in that incident."

Tears welled up in his eyes. He staggered over to the table and flopped into the chair. Sara glanced at his daughter. She was staring at her father wearing a frown.

"Dadda?"

Carla waved a doll in front of the girl to distract her. It didn't work. Emily scrambled to her feet and threw herself onto her father's lap. He hugged her and kissed Emily's tiny face over and over as the tears rolled down his face.

"Dadda, why you cwying?" Emily asked, her petrified gaze darting between Carla and Sara.

"Daddy's upset, sweetie. Go play with your toys. I'll be all right. Go with the nice police lady, there's a good girl." He tried to push his daughter off his lap, but Emily flung her arms around her father's neck, determined to hang on to him. Defeated, he buried his head in her neck and sobbed. Little Emily smoothed a hand over her father's cheek, her own cries soon turning into an anxious scream.

Sara watched the scene with a huge lump in her throat. At one point she had to turn away from the father and daughter to wipe away a tear. She noted Carla was struggling to hold back the emotion as well. Sara was desperate to go; however, she was aware how leaving a grieving family in this state would come across.

"Brian, is there someone we can ring for you?" Sara asked.

"My mother." He rang the number on his mobile and passed her the phone. "She's called Sharon."

A woman answered soon after it started ringing. "Goodness me, give me a chance to get in the door, Brian."

"Sorry, Sharon. This is DI Sara Ramsey. I'm with your son at his home. He's asked me to call you. Is there any chance you can pop over?"

"Oh my! Whatever is the matter? He was okay when I left half an hour ago. Has something happened?"

"Please, Sharon. If you could come soon, that would help."

"I'll get my shoes on and be right over." The woman ended the call before Sara could either say goodbye or caution her to drive carefully.

"What am I going to do without her?" Brian whimpered between sobs. He kissed Emily on the cheek and crushed her to him, her own sobs coming out as short, sharp gasps now.

Sara was at a loss for words, memories she thought she'd successfully pushed to the back of her mind suddenly resurfacing. She knew what this man was about to go through over the coming weeks and months—a great sense of loss she wouldn't wish on her worst enemy. The statistics surrounding the loss of a loved one in this situation weren't good. She'd been one of the lucky ones and hadn't had any suicidal tendencies. This man would need the assistance and love of the rest of his family to overcome the trauma lying ahead of him and his young daughter.

A few minutes later, the front door opened and a chubby woman wearing brightly coloured spectacles appeared in the doorway. She rushed across the room to be by her son's side. Her granddaughter reached up her hands for a cuddle. The woman bent down and gently removed Emily from his lap. "Should I sit down to hear this?"

"I think it would be wise," Sara agreed, pulling out a chair next to her son. The woman reached for his hand. "I'm ready. It's Tina, isn't it? Don't tell me she's gone."

Sara nodded. "I'm afraid so. There was an incident in town. Your daughter-in-law lost her life."

The woman constantly shook her head, disbelief swimming in her eyes as the tears fell. "This is awful. You said an incident, not an accident. What do you mean by that?"

Sara glanced down at Emily sitting on her grandmother's lap. "It's hard to reveal what occurred. The last thing I want to do is upset Emily further."

Brian sighed. "We need to know. Emily doesn't understand. She's upset because we're upset. She's too young to realise what's going on. Please, we have to know how Tina di..." His hands covered his face and he sobbed.

Sara left it a few seconds until his sobbing subsided, then she told the family about the moped driver's part in their relative's death.

"She was targeted? Is that what you're saying?" Brian asked, his eyes creased in confusion.

"Maybe. I think the main reason for the attack was her handbag."

"He took that, didn't he?"

Sara nodded. "Yes. It would appear that wasn't enough for him. If he'd driven off, I think Tina would still be with us today."

"Do you know the driver? Did you get his number plate?"

"No. All we can say at this point is that this week alone a few incidents have come to our attention where mopeds have been the only form of transport involved."

"Why haven't you caught the bas...the idiot then? If you know he's involved, it's a no-brainer from where I'm sitting."

"Without the benefit of having a readable number plate, we're at a loss to know more about the driver. My team are working hard on the information provided to us. I assure you, we will catch the person responsible soon."

"Go, get out there and find him then," Brian instructed, leaping out of his chair.

"I'm going to leave you a card. Ring me if you need any assistance with anything."

Brian marched through the house, expecting them to follow him.

"He's angry, I'm sorry. Please find this person. If they're intentionally targeting women or people in the city, they need to be locked up."

"We're doing our best. Please try and get Brian to see that. I understand his anger; I lost a loved one in similar circumstances. He's striking out, which is only natural. Take care, Sharon."

"Thank you, Inspector. Will you keep us informed?"

"I'll definitely do that."

Sara and Carla left the room. Brian was holding the front door open for them, his head bowed in what appeared to be shame.

"We'll be in touch soon, Brian. Again, my condolences for your loss."

"Thank you. I'm sorry for my outburst. Goodbye, thank you for coming here to tell me in person."

"You're welcome. Take care of yourself and your daughter."

Outside, Sara walked Carla back to her car in silence.

Carla unlocked her door and slid behind the steering wheel. "You look as if you need a drink. A stiff one at that."

Sara shook her head. "All I want to do is go home and snuggle up to my cat. Today has summoned up memories I'd rather not have to deal with. Enjoy the rest of your evening. See you around eleven, although I'm sure I'll show up earlier than that."

"See you then. Hopefully, some more information will come our way to nail these bastards. I forgot to mention it back at the station, what with the chief being there."

"What's that?"

"Did you notice the helmet used by the moped rider was different to the others?"

"I hadn't, no. Okay, that's something we'll need to look into tomorrow. Goodnight, love. Drive safely."

"You, too. Try not to dwell on your past too much tonight. You've been doing so well lately, it would be a shame to ruin it now."

"I won't allow that to happen. Thanks for caring." Sara stood and watched her partner drive away, the evening chill raising the hairs on the back of her neck—or was it?

She spun around, sensing someone was watching her. When the coast appeared clear, she chastised herself and jumped in her car, engaging the central locking as soon as she got in.

"You're imagining things." Starting the car, she began her twenty-minute journey home, shuddering a little as she set off. Even turning the heater on full blast did nothing to shift the sense of foreboding wrapped around her shoulders. She constantly searched her rearview mirror—nothing.

Behave! There's nothing out there. It's been a long day, week. My mind is playing tricks on me.

She'd finally managed to convince herself that her tiredness was behind her twitchy behaviour. That was until she pulled up outside her house. She slammed on the brakes and stared at the message scrawled in red paint across her front door.

Slag! You're Gonna Die!

What the actual fuck is that about? Who? More to the point, why? Why would anyone do that to my door?

She gasped, realisation dawning on her faster than a bolt of lightning. Someone was watching her. Was this to do with her relationship with Mark? It had to be with the word *slag* at the beginning of the threatening message.

Do I call it in or deal with it myself? How long has my door been like that? All day, or has someone dropped by this evening, in the dark, to carry out the bloody upsetting deed?

No amount of questions led to the truth. She was pissed off that someone had treated her brand-new house so appallingly, threatened her happy environment—on a whim? She shook her head.

Nope, a lot of thought had gone into this, that much was evident. But who? Who was going out of their way to make her life uncomfortable? She parked the car, grateful she had a garage, even if it was chock-full of damn boxes still. She made a mental note to sort that out at the weekend. Until then, she'd have to risk the car outside and hope the vandals had done enough damage for one day. Two incidents within the past twenty-four hours were enough, weren't they?

Sara walked up the path to the front door, key in hand. She ran a finger through the red message and gasped. *It's still wet.* She spun around, her heart pounding violently against her ribcage. Her breath came out in sharp, short bursts. There was no one around. A car drew up outside one of her neighbours'. The man left his vehicle, glanced her way for the briefest of moments then dashed inside his house. *Was that guilt or embarrassment flashing across his face?*

She rushed inside. Misty immediately wrapped herself around her legs in a figure of eight. She took time out for a few seconds to cuddle her furry companion before removing her coat and jacket, then she dashed into the kitchen where she ran a bowl of hot water and retrieved the sponge she kept under the sink which she used to clean her car. She raced outside and slammed the front door shut behind her. "Ah, fuck, my keys are in my damn pocket. What a frigging idiot I am." Her anger increased when she realised that her phone was in her coat pocket as well. There was nothing for it, she'd clean off the damn door and knock on one of her neighbours' doors to ring her father. Her parents had a spare key to her house, but it was vitally important for her to clear up the damage the mindless idiot had caused first.

Some parts were tougher than others to remove. She put that much effort into scrubbing the door clean that she neglected to feel the cold as the temperature plummeted around her. Sweat beaded on her forehead as she dipped the sponge one final time into the cooling water. She stood back to admire her hard work and then rushed to the end of the path and threw the red-stained water down a nearby drain.

That put a dent in their plan. Now, how the heck do I prevent it from happening again?

No sooner had she thought of her dilemma, than the solution came flooding through her mind. "I'll get a home surveillance camera fitted. Dad should be able to do that for me."

"Evening. Do you make a habit of talking to yourself?" a man in his fifties she recognised as living in the house three doors up from her asked, startling her.

She covered her heart with a damp hand. "Sorry, I didn't see you there."

"Obviously. I didn't mean to startle you. Ex-boyfriend do that?" He motioned to her front door with his chin.

"Not likely. I don't suppose you saw anyone hanging around here earlier, did you?"

"No, I only came home thirty minutes ago. Took Muffin here for a walk as soon as I got in. If it helps, the damage was done by then. It couldn't have been on there long, not if you've successfully managed to get every last bit off. There are some sick shits out there. Excuse my language."

"You're excused. I couldn't agree with you more. Umm...I hate to ask, but in my rush to clean up, I left my keys inside. It wasn't until I shut the door that I realised. I don't suppose I could use your phone, could I? To ring my father to come and rescue me."

"Of course. Shut your phone inside, too, did you?"

Embarrassment heated her cheeks. "You got me."

"Come on then. Let's get you out of the cold and into the warm."

Sara smiled, dropped the bowl on her doorstep and jogged to catch up with the man. "Thanks, I truly appreciate this."

"No problem. Tell me it's none of my business if you like...The missus and I were wondering what type of job you do. I mean, you always look smart when you set off." He held up a hand to stop her from answering. "No, don't tell me, I reckon you're a PA to a high-flying executive."

She chuckled, a sudden desire to be just that flashing through her mind. "And what does your wife reckon?"

"She thinks you're either a doctor or a surgeon at the hospital." He opened the back door and pulled his dog out of the way. "Ladies first."

"Thanks. Sadly, you're both wrong. I'm a detective inspector with the West Mercia Police."

His eyes widened, mimicking large dinner plates. "Wow, I'd never have put you down as a copper. Shit! Oops, I apologise for my language again, and someone had the audacity to daub that distasteful message on your front door? Shame on them. I hope you catch them and throw the bloody book at them."

She leant in and whispered, "So do I. I might treat them to a stretch on the rack down in the police cells first, though." She laughed when his eyes shot even wider.

"What? You have a torture chamber down at the nick? I didn't know that."

A female appeared from the hallway, laughing. "Ted, you can be so gullible at times."

"Me?" He pointed to his chest, his gaze drifting between his wife and Sara.

"Yes, you. Hello, dear. I've been watching you get rid of that filth. You're lucky it hadn't dried. I think you would have possibly needed a new front door if that had been the case. I'm Mavis, by the way. Would you like a cuppa? You must be perished, doing all that out there with no coat on."

"Thanks, Mavis, you're very kind." She held out her hand to the man first. "DI Sara Ramsey." Ted shook it with vigour then Sara shook his wife's. "Pleased to meet you, Mavis. I can't thank you enough for helping me out this evening."

Ted waved a dismissive hand. "Isn't that what neighbours are for?"

She smiled. "Not always. I appreciate your kindness."

"I'll get the phone for you." Ted left the room and returned carrying a portable phone moments later.

In the meantime, Mavis put the kettle on and was busy getting the mugs ready for their drinks.

"Have you settled in okay?" Sara asked.

"Just about. It takes time, doesn't it? Must be hard for you, unpacking all those boxes while working all day. I'm only part-time, a school dinner lady, for my sins, at the local primary school."

"Rather you than me." Sara laughed.

"It's not such a bad job. Gratifying to know that sometimes the school is supplying some of the kids with their only cooked meal of the day."

"That's very sad. I had two main meals when I was growing up. Lord knows how I didn't end up the size of a house."

Mavis raised a hand and pointed her index finger. "I know why. I bet you were involved in a lot of outdoor activities after school, am I right?"

"You're good. Yes, I was captain of the girls' netball team."

"I could tell. There's not an ounce of fat on you. What do you do to keep fit now?"

Sara's mouth turned down at the sides. "Nothing. Except the odd jog. I need to get back into a routine. I used to do a lot of cross-country running and walking in the hills when I lived in Liverpool."

"Liverpool? What made you come here?" Mavis asked, pouring the water into the mugs. "Sorry, don't mind me. Make your call, we can have a natter afterwards."

"Thanks." Sara dialled her parents' number. "Dad, I'm in desperate need of your help."

"Crikey, what's wrong, love?" her father asked, his tone tinged with concern.

"I've locked myself out. Can you come and rescue me, please?"

"Oh, is that all? I thought something major had happened then."

If only you knew. But I have no intention of telling either you or Mum what is going on in my life at present. She'd intentionally kept the text message a secret from them and now she'd do the same regarding the message scrawled across her front door. They'd only worry if she didn't.

"I'll be there shortly. Can you wait somewhere out of the cold until I get there?"

"The neighbours have kindly taken me under their wing. There's no rush, I'm having a cuppa with them. Twenty minutes will do, Dad."

"That suits me. See you then. I think your mother knocked you up a couple of pasties today. I'll bring them with me."

"Sounds yummy. Thank Mum for me. See you in a little while." She ended the call and passed the phone back to her host, Ted. "You've just saved my life without realising it. Looks like dinner is on the way, too."

They all laughed.

"Take a seat. Can I get you a chocolate biscuit to keep you going?" Mavis asked, setting the three mugs on the round pine table.

"I better not, thanks all the same. Are you local?"

"Not far. We've come from Worcester. Always yearned to live in the Wye Valley. This was the closest we could get for our money. Still, it's not far away. You said you came from Liverpool. Was that to move closer to your parents?"

"Yes and no. Tragedy struck my life a couple of years ago. I lost my husband in a gangland shooting. It dawned on me how much I missed Mum and Dad and the rest of my family. Both my brother and sister live in Herefordshire. It wasn't a hard decision to leave Liverpool once Philip passed away."

Mavis placed her hand over Sara's. "How dreadful. I didn't mean to open old wounds." She smiled at her husband whose head had dropped a little. "We lost our daughter last year. She was on a gap year from university and decided to go backpacking around Australia."

"Oh no. What happened?"

Mavis gulped and pulled out a hanky from the box sitting in the centre of the table and dabbed at the tears that had formed in her eyes. "She was staying in a hostel, and one of the men took a fancy to her. Apparently, so witnesses said, she rejected his advances, and he drew a knife. Several men tried to help her, but the man held the knife to her throat and dragged her outside. He took the car keys off another man staying at the hostel—they all thought he was going to abduct her." She paused to take a sip of her drink then wrapped her hands around the mug on the table. "The men trying to help Susie were shocked when the man slit her throat and tossed her aside to get in the vehicle. They were too stunned to chase after him."

Ted sniffled and patted his wife's hand. "The saving grace is that she didn't suffer. According to the men who tried to help, she passed away within seconds. Although, that image of our beautiful daughter in the hands of a madman haunts us day and night."

"I'm so sorry for your loss. It's one of the reasons I didn't think twice about leaving Liverpool. The crime rates are escalating up there at an astonishing rate. I thought I'd move down here where it was quiet. That's a laugh. This week alone has seen a few gruesome crimes land on my desk for me to try to solve."

Ted shrugged. "It's the world we live in. I'm sorry someone defaced your front door with that filth. Had we seen anyone doing it, we would have intervened. Although speaking out while someone is in the actual act might have been a tad foolish on our part. Sometimes, a well-meaning shout of 'Oi, what the hell are you doing?' wouldn't go amiss."

"A couple of things have happened to me since I moved in. The thing is, I haven't got a clue who's likely behind the vandalism. Someone even poisoned my cat a few months ago. She survived, thank goodness, but it was touch and go for a while."

Ted and Mavis both shook their heads.

"What a cruel world we function in," Mavis replied, clearing her throat when the words caught on the way out.

A comfortable silence followed while they drank their drinks.

"Dad should be here soon. Sorry to have inconvenienced you both."

"Nonsense, it was a pleasure helping you out. I would hope you'd do the same for us if ever we found ourselves in your shoes."

"Absolutely, one hundred percent."

A horn beeped outside.

Sara downed the rest of her drink, patted Muffin the poodle on the head and left the table. "Thank you again. Sorry it's taken me so long to make your acquaintance."

"You're a busy lady. Promise me you'll give us a shout if ever you need our help in the future."

"I promise, and vice versa. If there's anything I can do to help you out, don't hesitate to batter down my door—that is if it's not covered in red paint." She laughed, trying to make light of the situation, and exited the back door to find her father waiting in the doorway of her home.

Misty escaped the front door. Sara quickly pinned her to the ground and took her inside.

She kissed her father on the cheek. "Thanks for coming over, Dad. I'm going to keep Misty in now the nights are colder. She can use the box instead."

"Sorry, love. I didn't know. I would have kept a closer eye on her had I known. Fancy shutting yourself out. How did that happen?"

Sara had to think of a plausible excuse quickly to combat her father's suspicious nature. "I was ferrying some work in and closed the front door behind me. The wind must have caught it, and bingo, the damn door shut firm. Luckily, Ted was walking past and invited me in for a cuppa and offered the use of his phone."

"That was nice of him. Well, I better get back to your mother. She hates being alone in the house after that last case you worked on."

"Tell her not to worry, Dad. That was a one off, you know murders rarely happen in our neck of the woods."

"I wish I had your optimism, love. We never dreamt it would happen in the first place, but it did. Are you sure you're going to be okay?"

She kissed him and noticed the parcel he'd placed at the bottom of the stairs for her. "Of course. Stop worrying. Thank Mum for the pasties. I think I'll have one with a tin of beans for my dinner."

He wagged a finger. "Your mother would tell you off for not eating enough vegetables. As you know, I'm rather partial to a can of baked beans myself now and again, even if the side effects are a little unforgiving."

She chuckled. "Goodnight, Dad. Give my love to Mum."

He waved and then blew her a kiss and slipped into the car. He wound down his window. "See you soon. Come over for the weekend. Timothy and Lesley are both coming over. It would be nice to have you all under the same roof once in a while."

"I'll ring you tomorrow, Dad. I'm working a hectic case right now and not sure about making any arrangements that I might not be able to keep."

"Do that. Make it if you can, love."

He did a three-point turn in the road and waved as he passed the house. Sara shut and locked the front door, ensuring the safety chain was attached. Her nerves jangled when it dawned on her that she was alone in the house, except for Misty, of course. She shook out her arms, trying to rid herself of the sudden build-up of tension and picked up the parcel from the stairs.

Sara put the oven on to warm—her mother's pastry was too good not to want it crispy—then she fed Misty. In a daze, she waited for her dinner to heat up while watching her cat eat. A tornado circulated her mind, followed by dozens of questions. Why was someone singling her out? Well, not just her. Mark was included in the scenario as well, but why? She didn't recall ticking off any of the neighbours. As far as she was concerned, everyone kept to themselves. Tonight, was the first time she'd struck up a conversation with any of them; therefore, that option could be discounted.

Leaving her to believe that it must be the gang they were trying to track down. She recalled having the sensation that someone was watching her back at the Chorley's house, although she hadn't spotted anyone in the vicinity. Walking through the house, Sara entered the lounge and went to close the curtains. Something caught her eye. She dashed back into the hallway, riffled through her handbag for her pepper spray, slipped on her shoes and rushed out of the front door. By the time she arrived at the spot she thought she'd seen someone, they'd gone. *Did I imagine it? Willing there to be someone here?*

Feeling dejected, she entered her home again and replaced the safety chain on the door. Stepping into the kitchen, she received an almighty fright when the alarm went off on the oven. After stirring the beans on the stove, she switched off the oven and dished up her dinner. Misty, ever keen on having a cuddle, followed her into the lounge. Sara was halfway through her much-needed meal when her mobile rang. As soon as she saw the name on the screen, she knew she should have ignored it, except that type of thing wasn't really in her nature.

"Hello, Charlotte, how are you?"

Phil's mother was the needy kind. Keen to hang on to the past, never willing to move forward.

"Missing you, dear. Thought I'd ring up to see how you were. We haven't been in touch for at least a month, maybe it's longer than that. I don't know, one day seems to go into the next with me. How are you?"

"Busy. Long day today. I've only just got home. I'm having dinner now."

"Oh my. I won't keep you long then. I wondered if you'd like to come over for dinner on Sunday. Donald will be here. It would be nice if you could make it."

Sara sighed. "No can do this weekend, Charlotte, I'm so sorry. I have a prior engagement."

"Oh! Don't tell me you're seeing someone?" she asked, sounding shocked.

"No. We're having a family get-together at Mum and Dad's. It's my sister's birthday." The last part was a lie, but she had to think up a reasonable excuse after Charlotte had snapped at her.

"Ah, I see. Sorry to jump down your throat. I should have known you wouldn't replace Phil so quickly."

Quickly? It's been over two years! "He'll always hold a special place in my heart, Charlotte, you know that. Have a lovely weekend all the same. I'll be in touch soon."

"Wait. If you can't make it this weekend, why don't you come over next weekend instead? We'd all love to see you."

"Can I get back to you on that one? It's just I'm in the middle of an important case, one that has meant I've had to alter my shift pattern around, starting from tomorrow. I have no idea what will be happening in twenty-four hours let alone in ten days' time."

"Very well," Charlotte said, a little too sharply for Sara's ear. "I'll leave you to finish your dinner. Ring me when you're less busy, the invitation still stands. We'd love to see you, and soon."

"Give my love to Jonathon. I'll be in touch sometime next week, I promise."

Charlotte hung up without even saying goodbye, proving how pissed off she was.

Sara replaced her phone on the arm of the couch and picked up her fork. A few seconds later, a text message came through. It was from Donald, Phil's brother, with whom she'd shared an awkward kiss a few months earlier, prior to meeting Mark.

HI, looking forward to seeing you next weekend. It'll be wonderful to catch up after all this time. I've missed you. Donald. x

SHE CLOSED her eyes and expelled a large breath. She had a feeling the Ramsey family were conspiring something between them. Something she was reluctant to be a part of. Why couldn't they just leave her alone, allow her to repair her own heart? She was successfully doing that with Mark, wasn't she? A smile pulled her lips apart. She put her plate on the floor beside her and reached for Misty. "Come here, you, give your old mum a cuddle." Misty purred loudly and rubbed her head under Sara's chin. "You like Mark, don't you? I am doing the right thing seeing him, aren't I?"

Misty's continual rubbing and purring was all the reassurance she needed from her treasured companion. Life was good, wasn't it?

CHAPTER 8

"Right, is everyone clear on what we need to do next?" Chris said, surveying the rest of the gang members in the living room.

"How many times do we have to go over this? You got doubts, Chris?" Tory challenged, taking a swig of beer from his can.

"I've always got doubts. You guys seem to be doing what you want lately, drawing unnecessary attention to yourselves."

Tory laughed until his head tipped back. "Yeah, right. Says you. Everything we do is planned out by you."

"Bollocks. I didn't tell you to kill that woman with the bus."

Tory took a step towards him and prodded him in the chest. "Don't give me that bullshit. Not after what you did to that girl's mother."

Chris cast an eye in the direction of Siobhan, sound asleep in the bed in the corner. "I didn't know she was going to follow us."

"Shit happens, right? I didn't know the frigging wench was going to step off the bloody kerb, but she did."

Fran cleared her throat. "Guys, we've made mistakes, we're all guilty of that. Why do we have to keep going over old ground all the time? It's not getting us anywhere, is it?"

Chris nodded. "Fran's right. We need to get our shit in order if this next part of the plan is going to work. This is the important part. If we fuck this up, we can say goodbye to our payday."

"We won't screw it up," Tory assured him.

Chris looked over at Fran and Mick. Sensing all wasn't right between the husband and wife team, he asked to see Fran in the kitchen. "Help me make a drink, Fran."

She glanced her husband's way. He nodded for her to go with Chris.

He shut the door once they were both in the kitchen. "Take a seat, Fran."

She lowered herself into the chair and ran an agitated hand over her face. "What's up, Chris?"

"I was about to ask you the same thing, love. I know when something isn't right. That's the vibe I'm getting from you and Mick tonight. Look, if you're not okay with the plan, then you need to speak up. Everyone has had the opportunity to speak out if they don't feel comfortable. What's going on?"

She let out a shuddering breath. "It's nothing to do with the plan as such. Shit, how do I say this? I never meant for it to happen."

Chris frowned and scratched the back of his neck. "You're not making any sense. What's going on?"

Fran raised a hand to her mouth and chewed on her thumbnail. Chris reached across the table and gently eased her hand away from her mouth.

"Tell me, what's bugging you?" he repeated.

"It's the girl."

"Which one in particular?" he asked, aware that Fran was in charge of feeding all the kids in their possession.

"Siobhan. My heart is breaking for her."

"You can't think like that, Fran. All of those kids are in the same predicament."

"I dispute that. The others didn't see their mother die in front of them."

He ran a hand through his cropped black hair. "I know, that was unfortunate."

"That's one word for it. Shit, man, can you imagine the trauma she's going through? It wouldn't be fair to palm her off onto someone else, knowing what might be going on in her head. I'm telling you, it'll only cause more strife in the long run if you ship her out with the others."

Stunned, Chris asked, "What are you suggesting?"

Fran's gaze dropped to her clenched hands on the table. "Well, Mick and I have discussed it at great length, and we're willing to take her. Adopt her as our own. She likes us. She's comfortable with us."

Chris stood and tipped his chair over. "Jesus, no way. That wasn't part of the plan. We need her to make up the numbers for the transaction to go through."

"So, nick another child," Fran replied with a glare.

"Not this close to the deadline. We've caused enough trouble over the last few days. My guess is the police in the city are going to be more vigilant in the future. You've already seen the warnings they've given out to parents to keep a closer eye on their kids. What makes you think it's going to be easy to swipe another kid off the streets?"

"Get a life, Chris. How the fuck have we managed to pick up the others? Parents ain't bothered where their sprogs are most of the time."

"True. I'm just saying that the pigs are gonna be on the lookout more at the mo."

"All right, I hear you on that. We'll go out of the area to achieve what we need in that case. There's always a way around things, if you're willing to go the extra mile. I am for that kid. Mick and I will go out and snatch another one if it means we can have Siobhan full time."

"This is nuts and wasn't part of the plan, Fran. I thought you hated kids?"

She shook her head furiously. "No! I've never been fortunate enough to have them. Most kids I can't bear to be in the same room as them. You think because I'm a woman that the instincts to care for them comes naturally? It doesn't."

"Now you're confusing me. Why is the new girl any different to the others in your care?"

"I've told you. The only reason I can give you is that she saw her mother die. Put yourself in her shoes for a second. How would you react?"

"It's an unfortunate situation, granted. Okay, look at it from another way. What if you get caught with the girl? She's old enough to realise what's going on. What if you're walking down the street one day and she screams that you're not her real mother and that you abducted her? Have you thought about that?"

Fran fell silent. She reached for the salt pot on the table and twirled it between her fingers. "We'll cross that bridge if it ever happens."

"You haven't thought this through properly. The child will always remember her mother and the fact she was abducted. Can you seriously live with the consequences of your actions? Knowing that she could take off at the drop of a hat? Run off to try and find her father? Talking of which, he's not likely to give up the search for her, is he? No father who truly loves his child will ever stop searching for her. That's why she has to leave the country. Go with the other kids on their journey."

Fran clutched a hand to her chest and glanced up at him with bulging tears threatening to fall. "You're not listening to me, to what's going on in my head and my heart. I love her, Chris. I'll do just about anything to keep her, we both will."

Chris inclined his head. "Whoa, is there some kind of veiled threat in that sentence?"

"No. Not at all. I didn't mean I would do anything to dob you in. All I was getting at is that Mick and I will do what's necessary to replace the child as we've already discussed."

"And I've told you that sort of thing comes with risks. This whole plan has taken six months to put in place, and now you're teetering on the edge of making a mockery of all we've done. For what? The love of a kid who will probably go on to despise you in a few years?"

"Mick and I have gone over this. It's not a whim, I swear. Please,

Chris, don't deny us this opportunity. Once we've got another kid to replace her and the transaction has gone through, my husband and I are going to live in Ireland. His father left him a small house out in the sticks. I'll home-school her if I have to, to keep her safe."

"While I admire your willingness to do the right thing by the child, I still think you're making a huge mistake."

"One that we're willing to make, given the chance. Only you can give us that, mate. I'm begging you to let us do this."

Chris threw his hands up in the air. "Shit, I repeat, this wasn't part of the plan. I'm far from happy about it. We're going to have to run it past Tory. If you think I've just given you a hard time, it's nothing compared to what I anticipate he's gonna do."

She left her chair and ran into his arms, planting tiny kisses over his face. "Thank you. Thank you."

He grabbed both her wrists and smiled down at her. "I wish you well in the future, Fran. Without you caring for the kids over the past six months, none of this would have been possible. Now get to work, I need a coffee."

"Go on, I'll bring it through in a moment."

He left Fran humming as she filled the kettle. He had no intention of telling the other two about the conversation they'd held; however, seeing Mick's face and the anguish etched into his features when he entered the room, it was clear the big man knew exactly what had taken place. He smiled at Mick and crossed the room to check the girl. *She's lucky to have Mick and Fran as parents.*

Fran brought in four mugs of coffee.

Everyone accepted a drink except Tory, who raised his can of beer. "I'll stick with this."

Chris sipped his coffee and then announced, "We have a change to the plan."

"What the fuck are you talking about?" Tory demanded angrily. "Not five minutes ago we agreed the plan was a good one."

"Things have changed since then."

"In what frigging way? Come on, out with it."

Chris glanced at Fran and raised his eyebrow. "Do you want to tell him? She's asleep, by the way."

Fran glanced past him to see for herself if Siobhan was asleep or not. "I just had a chat with Chris. Mick and I want Siobhan for ourselves."

"What? You don't even like kids! This is frigging insane." Tory collapsed onto the couch.

"We still have time before the transaction takes place to pick up another child. Neither you nor Chris have to get involved. The onus is on us to pull it off." She smiled at her husband.

Mick offered her a half-smile in return. "We love her. She's been through enough in her young life. She deserves some happiness."

Tory shot out of his chair again and pointed at Mick. "For fuck's sake, have you frigging heard the crap spilling out of your gob? She deserves some happiness? With the bastards who abducted her and kept her chained to a bed?"

Chris had a feeling Tory would react like this. "Mate, you need to calm down."

Tory took two strides and was in his face. "And you need to put a stop to this before this whole fucking thing explodes in our faces. We're on a tight deadline, and you're allowing these two morons to start making up their own plans. This comes to an end now, or I'm out of here."

Fran went to stand by her husband and reached for his hand.

Chris backed up a few paces, away from Tory's stale breath. "We've got forty-eight hours before we have to hand the kids over. That gives Fran and Mick time to grab another sprog."

Tory shook his head. "Seems like you guys have it all sussed. How long have I been kept in the dark about this?"

"You haven't. Fran just told me in the kitchen. Let's give them twenty-four hours to pull it off, mate. Where's the harm in that?"

Tory shook his head and waved a hand in frustration. "You do what you gotta do. Don't include me in it. I want no part of it. I'm outta here."

Chris watched him go, unsure whether he should call him back or not. Instead, he felt it was best to leave him to mope. Fran started crying. Mick quickly crossed the room and gathered her in his arms.

He glanced at Chris. "Sorry, mate. We never intended this to happen. I know it's caused a bit of strife. The missus and I will put things right. I promise you."

Chris patted Mick on the back. "He's always going off on one, you know that. Let him calm down a bit, he'll come around eventually." *I hope. If he doesn't, then I'm not sure where that leaves us.* This was definitely the last job he intended doing with these guys. He'd take the money owing and retire somewhere warm away from them and his uncaring family. *They'd* driven him to do this. Their lack of empathy and love was the cause of the evil coursing through his veins.

It's about time they all know who they're dealing with.

CHAPTER 9

SARA SLEPT VERY little that night and rose at her normal time. Knowing that Mark was usually awake around the same time, she took a gamble and rang him.

His voice was groggy when he answered. "Hello."

"Hi, it's only me. Sorry, did I wake you?"

"Yes and no, I was dozing. Lying here thinking about you, if you must know."

"Really? Or are you just saying that?" she asked, chuckling like a hormonal teenager.

"I might be. How are you?"

She sighed. "This case has really taken hold. One of those cases that won't let you have any downtime. Sorry I didn't ring last night. Things were a little hectic when I got home."

"Care to elaborate on that? Not more vandalism?"

She winced, regretting her words. "No, nothing like that. It was just by the time I got home all I was fit for was falling into bed. I'm supposed to be starting my new shift today, but you can bet I'll go in at my usual time."

"That's a shame. You should be resting while you've got the opportunity. If I wasn't travelling today, I'd pop over to see you."

"What time are you setting off?"

"At eight-thirty. I better get up soon and pack my bag."

"You go. Sorry to disturb you. I'll see you when you get back."

"Hey, don't go. Will it be all right if I ring you while I'm away?"

Sara smiled and stretched out for Misty, drawing her in close for a cuddle, imagining her cat was Mark. "Of course. I probably won't get in until ten or later. You could always try and ring during the day. I might have to cut the call short if I'm dealing with something major, though."

"That's a deal. Either way, I'm going to miss not being able to drop round for a chat."

"Me, too. Looking forward to our date on Saturday."

"Always nice to have a date with a beautiful young woman to look forward to."

His compliment took the wind out of her sails. Had it happened a few weeks earlier, she would have run for the hills, waving her arms frantically impersonating a madwoman. "You're a charmer."

"I'm brave when there's distance between us. Not sure I'd have the courage to say it to your face."

Sara roared with laughter. It sounded as if they were more alike than she had first realised. "You're a scream. This suits me—nothing too heavy, right?"

"Right. Okay, I better jump in the shower and get on my merry way. Enjoy your lie-in."

"Thanks. Drive carefully. Ring me later, if only to let me know that you've arrived safely."

"I'll text you, how's that?"

"Perfect. See you on Saturday when you get back, Mark."

"Not sure how I'm going to cope until then, but I'm going to have to. Be safe out there."

"I will be. Enjoy your course." She ended the call, wondering if she'd done the right thing not telling him about the paint incident. A lightbulb went off in her head. She rushed into the bathroom to shower. After dressing and seeing to Misty's needs, she jumped in the car and headed into town to the local B&Q store. She asked a young

male assistant to help her. He took her to the right aisle and pointed
out what she needed. With the surveillance camera bought and sitting
on the passenger seat beside her, she drove home to read the
instructions.

She waved at Ted who rounded the corner towards his house.
"Morning Ted, how are you?"

He came to a stop with Muffin. "I'm fine. More importantly, how
are you?"

Sara held up the carrier bag and smiled. "I've been out shopping."

He frowned. "For anything in particular?"

In a hushed voice, she said, "A surveillance camera. All I have to do
now is figure out how to fit the darn thing."

"Ah, that's a good idea. I could lend a hand. Two brains are better
than one and all that."

"Would you? I'd hate to impose."

"You're not. I offered. All it will cost you is a mug of coffee. I'm
sure it'll only take ten minutes or so to install."

"I'd be grateful if you could. I'm hopeless with things like this."

He checked his watch. "Shouldn't you be at work or are you having
a day off?"

"I don't have to start until eleven today, that's why I thought I'd nip
into town to pick up this."

"Let me get some tools. You put the kettle on, and we'll have this
up and running in no time."

Ted was true to his word. Half an hour later, the camera was
installed, and Sara let out a relieved sigh to see it working.

"I can't thank you enough, Ted."

He waved away her gratitude. "That's what neighbours are for,
love—at least that's how it should be."

"Once this case is over and I have some spare time on my hands,
I'd love to invite you and Mavis to dinner."

"That sounds wonderful, although it's not necessary."

"Nonsense. That's a deal then. Thanks again, Ted. I'll feel a lot
safer now."

"Shame it's come to this. It'll act as a deterrent if nothing else."

"I better get ready for work now. See you soon, and thank you once again for taking care of me." She leant forward and pecked him on the cheek.

"Steady on now, we don't want to be the cause of any gossip. You're welcome, happy to help a damsel in distress."

"Mavis is lucky to have you."

"I'm the lucky one. Enjoy the rest of your day. Oops, should I say that to a copper?"

"It'll do." She smiled, waved farewell, closed the front door and watched him move away through the monitor in the hallway connected to her new gadget. *That'll stop someone in their tracks in the future, hopefully.*

THIRTY MINUTES later and Sara arrived at the station by the skin of her teeth.

Carla glanced up from her desk. "Only just made it. Everything all right, boss?"

"I'll tell you all about it in my office. A coffee would be nice."

Carla scraped her chair back and headed towards the vending machine.

"Anything I should be aware of?"

The team all shook their heads. Feeling discouraged, she continued into her office, hung up her coat and handbag and stared down at the pile of brown envelopes vying for her attention. Groaning, she picked up the first one as Carla walked into the room. "Thanks, Carla, take a seat."

Frowning, Carla did as instructed. "Sounds serious. Trouble?"

"Could be. I have no proof it was there, though. I didn't have time to think about taking a photo, and it was too late by the time I'd locked myself out."

Carla raised a hand to interrupt her. "Sorry, you're not making any sense. Can you rewind a bit?"

Sara pulled out her chair and flopped into it. "I apologise. Here's what happened when I got home last night." She filled her shocked partner in on the previous day's events and brought her up to date on installing the camera that morning.

"Bloody hell. Who do you think is behind this shit?"

Sara shrugged. "You tell me. Could it have something to do with the case?"

Carla shook her head slowly. "In my view, I don't think so. Not when the attacks have been personal. You could say that about Mark's car, too."

Sara leant her head back and expelled a large breath. "I have to put it aside for now and get on with the case. I'll let the DCI know later but I'm not about to waste any more of my valuable time trying to figure out who has a frigging grudge against me. It comes with the job."

Snorting, Carla said, "It's hardly a grudge. These are death threats you're receiving, not some form of playground snipes. Something needs to be done about it, boss."

"I am doing something. I've installed a camera at the house. My neighbours have promised to keep an eye on my home during the day when I'm not there—nice couple, they are. Lost their daughter in a tragic incident while she was backpacking last year."

"That's sad. Can you and Misty stay somewhere else for the next few days?"

"I don't want to be forced out of my home, Carla."

"I know. I'd feel the same. However, I'd be worried sick knowing that there are warped individuals staking out my house and causing damage. That takes guts, to target a serving police officer."

Sara let her partner's words linger for a few moments. "I'll think about it. My thoughts have to remain on the disappearance of these kids and the other cases we're dealing with. My problems don't match up to this crap, thankfully."

Carla's chin dropped onto her chest. "But they could do," she muttered.

"All right. I hear you. I've addressed the problem and will be cautious going forward. If you're having trouble dealing with it and want me to appoint someone else as my partner for a while, I wouldn't object."

Her partner's head shot up, and her gaze met Sara's. "No way! I'm with you through thick and thin, boss. I'm concerned about you, that's all."

"Okay, then bugger off and let me tackle this shit. I'll be out in twenty minutes whether I've completed this task or not. We need to recap on what we have and do some more chasing up today. Right?"

"I hear you. Always here if you need to vent."

"I know that." Sara smiled and watched her partner leave the office. Picking up the first brown envelope of many, she got stuck in and joined the rest of her team as promised, twenty minutes later.

"Crap!" Carla said, hanging up the phone and running an anxious hand through her hair.

Sara walked over to her desk and tilted her head. "What's wrong?"

"Another child abduction."

Sara kicked out at the nearby table. "Fuck. Where? It doesn't matter, tell me on the way. I'll get my coat. Tell Barry where the child was taken. Barry, you know the drill, get to it. Craig, you help him. Let's catch these bastards, and quickly." She rushed into the office, grabbed her coat and handbag and dashed through the incident room and down the stairs. Carla's heels clacked on the concrete behind her.

Within seconds they were sitting in the car, siren blaring, en route to the swing park on Aylestone Hill on the edge of the city.

"What happened?"

Carla sighed. "Apparently the mother was distracted, talking to one of the other mothers, thought her daughter was playing on the swings. When she looked up, the child was gone."

"Great. How difficult is it to keep an eye on your child nowadays? No, don't answer that, it was a rhetorical question. Winds me up something chronic that people can be so lax, especially when we've been putting out warnings to parents through the media. Do some people treat this parenting lark as one big joke? Again, don't answer that. I'm fucking annoyed and lashing out."

"Hey, I feel the same as you do, although I should imagine it's pretty difficult keeping your eye on a child twenty-four-seven."

"Yeah, it probably is. But if you're not up to the task then you have to take the responsible action and choose not to have them, like I have. I know I couldn't watch a kid like a hawk, be at their beck and call twenty-four hours a day."

Carla didn't respond. Instead, she glanced out of the window as they drove at speed to the location. "You're gonna have to calm down before you speak to the mother."

"I'm aware of that and I'll be as calm as I need to be by the time we get there. Here we are now." Sara inhaled and exhaled half a dozen times and then left the car.

There were a couple of squad cars at the scene, and four uniformed officers were taking down statements from the other mothers in the park. Sara tapped one of the officers on the shoulder and asked her to join her for a moment.

"Sorry, ma'am. The mother of the missing child is the one sitting on the bench over there. Her friend is comforting her."

"Thanks. You're doing a great job. Any witnesses so far?"

Disappointingly, the female officer shook her head. "No one saw a thing. So far anyway."

"Okay. Keep me informed if that changes. We'll have a chat with the mother."

Sara and Carla strode across the grass to the two women sitting on a bench, one of them sobbing her heart out. *A tad too late to have recriminations, love.* Sara winced, regretting her evil thoughts.

She produced her ID and announced, "Hi, I'm DI Sara Ramsey, and this is my partner, DS Carla Jameson. I take it you're the mother of the child?"

The woman looked up at them and sniffled, wiped her nose on a tissue and nodded. "Donna Parker. My little Lara has been snatched."

"How old is Lara?"

"She'll be six next week."

"Did you see the incident?"

"No. We...we were chatting."

"I see. How do you know the child was snatched? Perhaps she wandered off, have you thought about that?" Sara asked, her tone abrupt with impatience.

"Do you have to speak to her like that?" the woman's friend demanded, glaring.

"Like what? I'm concerned that Mrs Parker's child might have wandered off, and yet no one seems that bothered by it. Have you searched the area? Moved off this bench since the incident occurred?"

Carla grabbed Sara's arm and motioned with her head that she wanted a word. They stepped ten feet away from the two women.

"Boss, sorry to intervene, but you need to calm down. You're acting as though they're the guilty parties—they're not."

"You're wrong, Carla. They're just as guilty of failing the child. How do we know she hasn't wandered off somewhere? I want a search party up here immediately. We've got no witnesses to say that the child was abducted, so unless someone contacts us to say otherwise, we need to think of this case as the girl simply walking off. Am I wrong?"

"No. You're right, as always. I'll get on to the station now. My advice would be to go easier on the mother. She feels guilty enough as it is."

"Thanks for the advice. I'll handle things my way." Sara stomped back to the two women. "I'm sorry if I came across as abrupt. I'm concerned about the child. I've actioned a search of the area—it's important we don't treat this just as an abduction. We could be wasting valuable time. Your child could be close by. We need to check out the close proximity first. Has she ever wandered off before?"

"No, never. She has no reason to do that. Lara would never put me under unnecessary stress, she's not that type of child. I was distracted for a few moments, that's all. If she was still around here, she would have come back to me by now. Please, I know in my heart that someone has taken her."

"Okay, what I need is a recent photo. Do you have one on you?"

Mrs Parker withdrew her phone from her coat pocket and scrolled through her photos for one that would be suitable to use. She angled her phone at Sara a few times. Sara dismissed four until she finally showed her one that would look good on a TV bulletin.

"Thanks, that's perfect."

Carla arrived as Sara was taking a shot of the photo on her phone.

"Everything has been actioned, boss. The team should be here within twenty minutes."

"Good. I need to contact the station with this image of the child. I'll be back in a second. Can you take down the usual information, Carla? Any relatives in the area et cetera where the girl might have gone if she thought she was lost." She stepped away from the group again and rang the station. "Jeff, I'm sending you a photo of the child reported missing. Get it circulated ASAP, and do me a favour, get on to the TV stations. I want this girl's face plastered across every TV screen in the area by lunchtime."

"Leave it with me, boss. I'll ensure that happens. My guys should be with you soon."

"Good. Thanks, Jeff."

Sara ended the call and scanned the area ahead of the two women. Something wasn't sitting right with her, but she didn't have a clue what it was. Yes, she'd been harsh with the mother, but her child was missing, for fuck's sake. Something that should never happen. If it were left up to Sara, every child under the age of seven would be on one of those extending leads they used for dogs.

I know I'm being ridiculous. But heck, how many warnings do these parents have to bloody hear to get the message across? There are dozens of sick bastards out there, predators waiting to swoop on unsuspecting kids at any given moment.

Sara gestured for Carla to join her.

"What's up? What are you thinking?"

Sara shrugged. "To be honest, my mind is whirling out of frigging control. Let's get the search coordinated, and then I want to get back to the station. Without witnesses saying they saw something, it's a waste of time being here when we have other things to be getting on with. And no, that isn't me being harsh, it's a fact. The team are working on several avenues at the moment, and I have a feeling that I'm not willing to dismiss—that something big is about to break."

"Okay. I can't argue with your gut feelings, they're usually spot on."

"Glad about that. We'll action the search and get on the road within the hour. That'll give us enough time to question the other people, parents, in this park. Let's get on with it."

They split up and spent the next hour going from group to group. Some of the people had insisted they had to make a move, but Sara made sure they were all questioned thoroughly before they were allowed to leave the park.

A swarm of uniformed officers arrived in a police van. Sara instructed them to conduct a search of the immediate area of the park and the adjacent roads. She told them to report their findings back to Jeff, then she and Carla left the park and returned to the station. The mother looked none too happy, but that was tough. There were enough people searching for her daughter. Sara and her team had more pressing things to take care of.

When they arrived, Jeff brought her up to speed on what he'd accomplished, telling her that the girl's photo would be on the TV news within thirty minutes.

Sara smiled. "You're a legend, Jeff. Any calls you think I should know about, patch them through to my office."

"You've got it, boss."

Sara's legs were already weary as she climbed the stairs, even though her day had only just begun. She immediately headed for Barry's desk. "Anything on the CCTV?"

"There's a camera outside the park, none inside, unfortunately. I'm scanning all the vehicles, noting down things that don't sit well with me. Till now, I have an old escort and a white van. Craig knows that park well, tells me that a lot of tradesmen stop off there for their lunch which they purchase from the baker's up the road."

Sara raised a finger. "That's great information, except it's not lunchtime." She glanced up at the clock: almost twelve. "All right, it's coming up to it now, but it was earlier when the kiddie went missing."

Craig raised his hand to speak. "But if you start at five in the morning, boss, lunchtime could be at any time, if and when hunger strikes."

Sara nodded. "Excellent point. Okay, keep at it. Carla, you and I need to go over the evidence we have to hand already on the other cases. There are enough people working the Parker child case as it is. I think we're bloody missing something vital and need to find out what that is ASAP."

Carla nodded and lowered her voice to say, "Sounds like you've given up on the Parker child."

Sara vehemently shook her head and snatched a pile of A4 paper off the spare desk next to her. "My office when you're ready. A coffee would be nice, if you're buying."

Carla joined her, two coffees in hand, a few seconds later. "Sorry, did I overstep the mark?"

"Yes. I haven't given up on the Parker child. Like I said, there are a lot of bodies on that already. Therefore, I'd rather look back over what we have already, especially if there's a connection to the missing child. That's my train of thought anyway."

"Sounds good to me. Where do you want to start?" Carla placed the cups on the desk and sat opposite Sara.

"At the beginning. When we spoke to the officers in charge of all the missing children cases, I recall they all said the same. There were no witnesses to the crimes. It's as if the children just vanished, and yet they were all taken out in the open. How is that even possible?"

"Mind-boggling to me."

"Here's my thinking: we need to have a word with the kiddies' parents. I'm not saying that's going to be easy, but I think it's a necessity."

"What's your reasoning behind that, if you don't mind me asking?" Carla took a sip of her coffee.

"I'm searching for a link. While they might be random attacks, we shouldn't discount the kids being connected in some small way, or am I wrong about that?"

"No, I think you could be right. Is your intention to go and see the parents?"

Sara blew on her cup of coffee then took a sip. "Yep, I'd like to do that today, if possible."

"I'll make the necessary calls if that's how you want to proceed."

"Thanks. I need to keep on top of the team about the gym and moped angles. Again, I think we're missing something vital. Will you get Craig to contact all the moped suppliers within a fifty-mile radius for me? We need to know if any mopeds have recently been sold in the area, we already know where the helmets were purchased."

"I'll get on it right away. Anything else?"

"You deal with that, I need to contact the TV stations. I want them to run the CCTV footage of the Tina Chorley incident. Not the actual accident in which she lost her life, but the lead up to that. Let's shake the tree a little, see if anyone recognises that moped. I also want Lara's image prominent in the public's mind. I want them mentioning it every thirty minutes if necessary, until that child is returned."

"Does that mean you do think she's been abducted?"

"I haven't got a clue. It's called keeping our options open. I'm still really angry at the mother for not paying closer attention to her child. Can't people multitask these days? Keep one eye on the child whilst having a conversation with her mate?"

"I hear what you're saying. I think she'll do things differently in the future."

"You're assuming her kid will be returned to her. There's no guarantee there. Don't forget we're still trying to trace kids that went missing over six months ago."

"Fair point. Anything else?"

"That's enough to be going on with. You deal with that. I'm going to spend the next few hours going over the evidence file, see if anything leaps out at me."

Carla took her cup with her and left the office.

By the time Sara had flicked through the file, a headache was brewing. She took a paracetamol from her drawer and washed it down with the remains of her cold coffee that she'd neglected to drink.

It wasn't until later that day, at around seven, that a significant call came in to the incident room. Sara was doing the rounds with the team, keeping them on their toes.

Carla took the call and waved Sara over. She put the caller on speaker. "Mr Warren, would you mind repeating what you told me? My boss, DI Sara Ramsey, is listening to the conversation now."

The man groaned. "I said, I was walking my dog near the park where that lassie went missing today. It might not be anything, but I thought I'd ring up and let you know anyway. I saw a woman chatting to a little girl around that time at the park. She placed the girl in the back of a van—that's what I thought was weird. I know if the kid had been mine, I'd want her up front with me. The seats on those vans are long, aren't they? They can seat at least three people, as far as I can remember. It just struck me as being odd."

"I'm inclined to agree with you, Mr Warren. Did the van speed away from the park?"

"I don't think so. I'm not generally a nosy parker, sorry, I didn't take that much notice. It's just seeing the kiddie on the screen tonight, it got me thinking."

"Are you telling me you recognised the child?"

"Yes, sorry, didn't I say that? Bugger, that's my nerves playing up. It took a lot of courage for me to ring you lot. Not that I've got anything against you. I'm a model citizen who prefers to keep his nose clean."

"Okay, I understand. In that case, we really appreciate you getting in touch with us. Would it be possible for me to send a uniformed officer around to take down a statement?"

"Of course. I won't get into bother for this, will I? You know, if the people I'm ringing up about find out that I've dobbed them in."

"I assure you, there's no chance of that happening. Please don't lose any sleep over it."

"If you're sure. Mind you, I'm bound to lose sleep over that damn child. To think I could have prevented her going with that woman..."

"Would you recognise the woman again if you saw her?"

"I think so. The brain hasn't begun to fail me so far."

"Would you be willing to work with a sketch artist?"

"I don't see why not. Best do it quick while she's fresh in my mind.

Hey, my granddaughter is good at art. Maybe I can tell her what I saw and pass it on to you."

Sara chuckled at the man's enthusiasm. *Bless him.* "I'd rather do it in an official capacity, sir. These people are professionally trained and can alter things as they go along."

"All right. It's up to you, lovey. When shall I expect someone?"

"Christine, can you organise a sketch artist for me please?"

Christine nodded and picked up her phone immediately. "Mr Warren, will you stay on the line for a few minutes? We're organising things now."

"No problem. I'll hang on."

"Take down Mr Warren's address for me, Carla. I'll get the ball rolling with the desk sergeant."

Sara picked up the phone on a desk a few feet away and contacted Jeff who was still on duty. "Jeff, I've got a chap on the line who saw Lara Parker being abducted. We need to call off the search, and I'd like you to send one of your guys around to him to get a statement. I'm in the process of organising a sketch artist to attend, too."

"Sounds promising. I'll call it off now, ma'am. What's the man's address?"

Carla shoved a piece of paper in her hand. "Ten Forrest Hill, close to the park where the girl went missing, apparently."

"I know it well. Okay, leave it with me."

"You should be going home soon, right?"

"Thought I'd hang around for a bit until the search was called off. You know what it's like when there are kiddies involved, ma'am."

"I know. Okay, get yourself home now. See you tomorrow."

"Goodnight, ma'am."

Once Mr Warren was sorted and the sketch artist arranged to visit him in the morning, Sara went back to Barry and asked him to play the footage from the park over again.

"Stop. Let's focus on that van. I know what we're up against here. It's a white transit, the most common van there is in circulation, right? I get that—let's look for something distinctive about that van."

"You're not wrong, boss. We could be looking at thousands of the damn things. Jesus, millions even," Barry replied dejectedly.

"All right. No need to be overdramatic. I get your drift, though."

The phone rang again, and Carla answered it. "Mr Warren, yes, you did forget to mention that. Okay, I have the details down. We really appreciate you ringing back, sir. Goodbye."

Sara inclined her head, waiting for Carla to tell them what the old man had said. Her partner waved the piece of paper in Sara's face then snatched it back again before Sara could get her hands on the damn thing.

"Spill."

"He's only gone and given us part of the reg number."

"No! Really? The poor guy must have been more nervous than we realised, to forget to tell us about that. This is great. Okay, I need to calm down and breathe. Let's have it, Carla?"

"He got the last four digits, kicking himself he didn't note the rest of it down."

"That won't be a problem, will it, Barry?"

"It's better to work with something than nothing. Can someone else deal with that while I show the boss the footage?"

"I've got it," Christine shouted, attacking her keyboard like a woman possessed.

Sara squeezed Barry's shoulder. "Play it."

She, Carla and Barry, all watched the van pull into the entrance of the car park but not where it parked. That was where the footage of the van ended until the vehicle left a few minutes later.

"Anyone see anything we can work with?"

"Nope, it looks in reasonable nick to me, not that it matters now we have a partial plate number, boss. I think they've just nabbed their last kid."

Sara blew out a breath. "Let's hope you're right. I'm taking a punt on this. I'll get hold of Jeff and get him to circulate the details for uniform to be on the lookout for." She crossed her fingers, hoping to find Jeff still at his station. He was. She filled him in and told him what she wanted.

"That's great news. I'll pass on the details to the men on patrol, ma'am."

"Fabulous, now go home," Sara ordered, laughing.

"On my way out the door when you rang. I'll hang around for five minutes to action this then skedaddle."

Sara wished she could do the same. Her new shift wasn't due to finish for another few hours. There was still a lot for them to cover, even more so now with the information that had fallen into their laps.

CHAPTER 10

FRAN AND MICK arrived at the house before Tory showed up. They had achieved what they'd set out to accomplish and had another petrified kid in tow. She was crying, sobbing hard until she sat on the bed next to Siobhan. The pair held hands.

Siobhan smiled and told the new arrival, "It's alwight, they won't hurt us."

"What about your wrist?"

"It's getting betta, doesn't hurt so much now."

"All right. Enough chattering. Sit there and be quiet. Didn't your parents ever tell you that children should be seen and not heard?" Chris asked, a few paces away from the girls.

The children glanced at each other and back at him.

Siobhan shook her head. "Never heard that before, mister."

"Ha! It was drilled into me when I was two years old. That's the trouble in today's society, parents let the kids walk all over them. No discipline in place. You ever felt your fathers' hands on your backsides, girls?"

Siobhan and Lara clung to each other tighter and shook their heads.

"Right. Maybe if you had, you wouldn't be whining so much."

Fran grabbed Chris's arm and spun him around. "Leave them alone. Just because you were abused as a child, it doesn't mean we all were."

Chris unhooked her hand from his arm and took a few paces towards her. "Back off, Fran. If I ever need a lecture from you, I'll be sure to ask for one. You've got what you wanted, now get out of my face."

Fran walked away and mumbled something indecipherable.

He sprinted after her and yanked her around to face him. "If you've got something to say, be brave and say it to my face, got that?"

Mick shot out of his chair and grabbed him round the throat. The children both screamed.

Fran talked her husband down. "Mick, leave it. I can handle myself. What gives, Chris? Who has rattled your cage? Us? We've righted the wrong by getting another kid—give us a break, man."

Chris glared at Fran and then Mick. "You ever lay a hand on me again, big man, and you'll be sucking your food through a straw in the future, you hear me?"

Tory entered the room. "Oi, what the fuck is going on here?"

"Chris has lost the plot," Fran said before Chris had a chance to open his mouth.

"I have not. I'm anxious, that's all."

"We all are. We need to keep our shit together, not tear each other apart." Tory jabbed Chris in the chest as if to emphasise his point.

"Tomorrow is the drop-off. We need things to go according to plan or we're all fucked. Why don't we sit down and go over the details together one final time and forget about all this, deal?" Tory said, glancing around the other three members of the team.

"Fine by me," Fran replied, moving over to the table in the corner. "I need to feed the girls soon. Let's get on with it."

The three men sauntered across the room to join her. None of them looked in the mood for the meeting.

Chris started the proceedings off. "So, nothing has changed. The moped attacks have done what they were supposed to do and put the cops off the scent."

"Thank fuck for that, although I saw the kid's face plastered all over the TV today. That ain't gonna go down well when we do the exchange. The main man ain't gonna be happy," Tory warned them.

"Shit happens, right, Fran?" Chris said, forcing a grin.

"Get off my back, Chris. It'll all be good. Take my word for that."

Chris's eyes narrowed. "We'll see."

Tory punched Chris in the arm. "Let it go, man. They're gonna be the ones taking all the risks."

"That's right," Mick chirped up. "You two have the easy job in all this. We're the ones who have 'sucker' plastered on our foreheads."

Chris shrugged. "It makes it more plausible for a woman to make the drop-off. Do you want to swap places with either me or Tory, mate?"

"Nah, I'm with the missus all the way on this one."

"Then stop complaining," Tory warned.

Finally, Chris had some backup—it was obvious Tory was as narked as he was about the couple wanting to keep one of the kids. "So, you take the kids to the warehouse. George will give you the money once he's inspected them and he thinks they're up to scratch. If he doesn't like the packages, we're fucked. All you have to do then is drive back here and we split the money. Oh, and don't bring any attention to yourselves, no speeding et cetera. More criminals have been caught by doing something innocuous like that than anything else."

"And stop treating us as if we are the dumbest criminals to ever walk this earth, Chris," Mick barked, his anger distorting his features.

Fran placed a hand on her husband's arm to calm him.

Tory tutted, his annoyance obvious. "Don't start, guys. All this bad blood is likely to get us into trouble. Just think about the outcome. This time tomorrow we'll be back here counting the dosh."

"As I was saying…while you're dropping off the kids at six, Tory and I will be making a nuisance of ourselves in the centre of town. We'll be upping the ante on this one, keeping the police busy, going in the opposite direction to where you'll be heading. Anyone got any problems?" Chris glanced around the table.

The other three members all shook their heads.

"Everything is cool, man. We'll all meet up at five back here, right? We'll set off from here," Tory said.

"Why? Why do we all have to set off at the same time?" Mick pointed out. "What if the neighbours suspect something?"

"Like what? You guys are in and out of this place all the time, and they haven't suspected anything yet."

Mick shrugged at Chris's response. "Right, if there's nothing else to cover, I suggest we call it a day and get our heads down early. We've got the biggest day in our lives ahead of us. Fran, you said something about feeding the kids?"

"On it now. I brought a large pot of bolognese with me. All I've got to do is heat it up and put on a pot of pasta. Thought that would go down better than spaghetti."

"Will there be any left for us?" Mick asked, rubbing his rounded stomach.

"I always save enough for my honey." Fran tweaked his cheek and rose from the table.

"I'll go upstairs and check on the others," Chris said.

Chris left the room and went upstairs to the small room where they kept the other children. He walked into the main bedroom and opened one of the wardrobe doors which led into a secret room that was padded against any likely screams. He kept the kids in the dark, only switching on the light when they ate. He held his breath as he walked into the room. The stench from the buckets sitting by each of their beds where the kids went to the toilet burned his nostrils.

"How are you kiddies?"

The five girls all sat back on their beds, petrified he was going to hurt them.

"Ah, scared, are you? Never mind, you'll all be out of here tomorrow. You have a long drive ahead of you. At the end of that journey you'll be in your new homes." Excitement rippled in his voice at the thought of all the money heading his way. He didn't have an ounce of remorse for what he was about to do to the children. Why should he feel remorse? Kids had their uses in this life—they'd find out what those uses were once they were shipped out.

It made sense to ship them overseas. No chance of the girls being recognised on the streets of the UK then. Thousands of miles away, they'd learn to enjoy their lives. Maybe 'enjoy' was stretching the truth a little. Sold into slavery, some of them may lead better lives than they had with their parents. The parents who'd neglected them. Well, all except two of them. The two he'd specifically targeted to get his revenge—make that three, if you counted Siobhan. He rubbed his hands, a menacing grin parting his lips as the image of piles of money swam before his eyes. He'd be a wealthy man this time tomorrow. Now all he had to do was decide where to live out the rest of his life. Lying on a beach in Mexico had always appealed to him, drinking cocktails, a raven-haired beauty by his side. Sex on tap in a hut overlooking the ocean.

He walked out of the room again, leaving the light on so the kids' eyes were all adjusted by the time their meal arrived. In the kitchen he plunged a finger in the sauce and nodded, showing his appreciation.

"The kids could do with a bath during the day tomorrow. Fran, can you deal with that?"

"Already on my to-do list for the morning."

"Good. Glad everything is organised. Sorry for having a pop at you earlier."

Fran smiled. "You're forgiven. I know you didn't mean any harm."

With Fran back onside doing the dirty work in the morning, his day suddenly felt a lot brighter.

CHAPTER 11

CHRISTINE SHOUTED, whooping for joy. "I've got a possible match, boss, for the van."

Sara's heart pounded. She crossed the room and patted Christine on the back. "I knew you would do it. Okay, we need to think about this for a while. Put them under surveillance until we've got something more concrete we can use. In the meantime, I'm gonna take a gamble on it and get a warrant ordered. Give me the address, Christine?"

"It's eight Weatherfield Road. A Mick Granger."

"Great. See what you can find out about this man and anyone else sharing the house."

"Already started on that, boss. Hope to have something for you soon."

"Carla, get the registration number circulated for me. Tell the patrol vehicles not to apprehend but to report back to me personally if they spot it—doesn't matter what time of day or night."

"Will do."

Sara stopped at a free desk and started up the monitor. She pulled up a map of the local area. "Weatherfield Road, anyone know it?"

There was a lot of head shaking and no answers.

"Doesn't matter, I've got it. Well, what do you know? It's about half a mile away from where Siobhan was abducted and her mother was murdered."

"All right, but there was a moped involved in that incident, not a van," Carla was quick to point out.

"There has to be a connection. I'm willing to stake my career on that, Carla."

"Who am I to argue with that?" Her partner smiled. "Sorry to interrupt your flow, but our first meeting with the parents is at eight."

"Damn, I forgot all about that. All right, we better hit the road in that case. We can't do anything about the van until the warrant lands on my desk anyway."

"Do you want to put the van under surveillance?"

"Yep, we'll do that. Will and Craig, get over there. See if the van is at the address and keep an eye on it if it is. Report back when you arrive."

The two men nodded and rushed out of the incident room while tugging on their jackets.

Jubilation riffled through Sara. It was imperative for her to tamp down her enthusiasm and not get ahead of herself. There were still a lot of angles to the case that needed covering first before any likely arrests could be made. "What's our first stop, Carla?"

"Jessica Brams is the closest. She was also the first one I spoke to."

"Great, let's go see what she has to say. There has to be a connection that we're missing. I have a good feeling about this now. How about you?"

Carla waved her hand from side to side. "Borderline for me. Maybe I'm being a little bit cautious here."

"As we should be. You're right."

They left the station and eased through the traffic, surprised how light it was at this time of night. Sara drew the car to a halt outside a semi-detached house on a hill with a long front garden that had twenty or so steps leading up to the front door. She rang the bell. The outside light was on already. A woman in her early thirties, wearing jeans and a stripy jumper, opened the door.

"Hello, Mrs Brams, it's nice of you to see us. I'm DI Sara Ramsey, and this is my partner, DS Carla Jameson."

They both flashed their IDs for the woman to inspect.

"Come in. Go through to the lounge, first door on the right. My sister is in there."

Sara smiled and led the way through the hallway. Mrs Brams' sister was sitting on the leather sofa, awaiting their arrival. Sara nodded at the woman, who smiled at them both. But the smile only lasted a few seconds and was replaced by a look of concern.

"Can I get you a drink?" Mrs Brams asked.

"Not for us, thank you," Sara said. "Again, we appreciate you seeing us at such short notice. I realise it's been a while since anybody from the station has contacted you regarding your daughter…"

"Daughters," Mrs Brams corrected.

Sara turned to look at Carla who seemed as equally confused as she was. "I'm not with you, sorry. I was under the impression that you only had one daughter who was missing, Melinda Brams."

The woman nodded. "I have. My sister's daughter, Katrina Stone, was also taken. Sorry, I should have introduced you sooner."

"What? You're Mrs Fiona Stone and you're related?" Sara was astonished by the revelation.

"Yes. You were due to call at Fiona's after you'd visited me. We thought it would save you an extra trip."

"That's kind of you. Sorry, you'll have to forgive me for sounding dumbfounded, it's because I am. There is nowhere in the files I've been given to say that you're both related. This could throw a different light on things."

"In what way, Inspector?" Jessica Brams asked, sitting closer to her sister and reaching for her hand.

"We're looking for a connection, and you being related could lead us to that. Are you aware of the names of the other children reported as abducted?"

"Not really, no. Maybe that's me being selfish, only being concerned about Katrina and Melinda. What about you, Fiona?"

Her sister shook her head, her eyes welling up with tears. It was obvious to Sara that Jessica was the stronger of the two women.

"Okay, not to worry. I'm intrigued about the connection between you and the possible abductor. It's very rare for this to happen. Which leads me to believe your children's abductions could have been planned. Do you know anyone who could have done that? Have you fallen out with someone perhaps, over the years, who might think about getting their revenge?"

The ladies stared at each other for a long moment.

"I can't, no," Jessica replied.

Something about the look in Fiona's eyes made Sara suspicious. "Fiona, what are you thinking?"

Fiona's head dropped and then rose again when her sister placed a finger under her chin. "Say what's on your mind, love. No one is going to hold it against you."

"Aren't they? What if I'm wrong about this? We've discussed it dozens of times, and you think I'm barking up the wrong tree, but I know in my heart he has something to do with this."

Sara sighed, hating to disrupt the conversation between the two sisters but determined to get to the bottom of what they were both referring to. "Sorry to interrupt. If you have an inkling, you really ought to tell us, if only to eliminate that person from our enquiries."

Fiona turned to face Sara. "It could be our brother."

"What? What would lead you to think that?" Sara asked.

"Jessica thinks I'm wrong, but I have a gut feeling about this that I can't let go of."

"Did you mention this to the investigating officer at the time of the abduction?"

"No. Jessica persuaded me not to say anything. I can't sleep, haven't slept for weeks since Melinda went."

"Does your brother live locally?"

"Yes, not far from here," Fiona replied.

"The thing is, I don't believe he's capable of doing such a dreadful thing. He was out there searching for both girls. Would he really do that if he'd taken them?" Jessica said, biting her lip.

Sara nodded. "It's possible. He could have done that in order to avoid any attention landing on himself. May I ask why you believe he's behind this, Fiona?"

"Revenge. Pure and simple."

Jessica gasped. "No, I don't think so, you've got this all wrong, Fiona. Chris wouldn't hurt us in this way, not after all these years."

Sara raised her hand and pointed a finger. "Please, ladies, you need to tell us what has gone on in your past to make you want to suspect your brother of doing something so atrocious to his siblings."

"I can't say it," Fiona told her sister.

Jessica swept a shaking hand over her face. "Mum abused him as a child."

"Just him, or were you abused as well?"

"Just him. Fiona and I may have been slapped the odd time, but it was nothing compared to what Chris went through."

"Do you know why she turned on your brother like that?"

"My sister and I have discussed it a few times over the years, not lately, though. We believe that as Chris was the only boy, Mum took it out on him for Dad walking out on us."

"I see. So she directed the sins of the father onto the son, but never punished the girls in the family. Are there only the three of you?"

"Yes. We lost Mum six months ago."

Six months ago was when the first child went missing. Could his mother's death be the trigger that set the ball rolling?

Sara nodded, noting that Carla was looking at her and guessed the same thing was running through her partner's mind.

"When was the last time you had any contact with your brother? Sorry, what's his full name?"

"Christopher Moore, Chris. He lives at thirty-three Spinacre Road."

"Thanks for that. And the last time you saw him?"

"Three or four weeks ago for me," Jessica said, glancing at her sister.

"About the same. He hasn't rung me since I last saw him, not that he tends to do that much anyway."

"What's his relationship been like with you and your children over the years? Jessica, why don't you go first?"

"Mediocre at best. I've tried to right the wrongs, showed him how much he meant to us, but he's always kept his distance with his emotions. Shrugged off the past, if you like, and was never open to speaking about it."

"And you, Fiona?"

"Jessica was always closest to him. I'm the oldest. They're closer in age than I am, only by a couple of years, though. The thing is, all the time Mum was beating him, we stood back and let it happen. Too afraid to stick up for him. I remember when he left home at sixteen, he stood on the doorstep and pointed a finger at us both, swore blind that he would get his revenge one day."

"Despite that, you stayed in touch?"

"Yes. Although he never went near Mum again. Maybe he remained in touch to keep up with any news about Mum. Since her death, he's been coming around more."

Sara nodded. "Interacting with you and the children, playing the doting uncle, that type of thing?"

"That's exactly how it was," Jessica said quietly. "Was he trying to get on our better side, is that what you're suggesting?"

"Sounds like it to me," Sara admitted. "It's not uncommon for people with an agenda as vile as this to change their ways to suit the circumstances. To avoid their nearest and dearest becoming suspicious."

"What will you do now?" Jessica asked, clutching her sister's hand tighter.

"We'll need to go and see him, see what he has to say for himself."

"Oh gosh, you won't mention us, will you?" Fiona asked, her bottom lip trembling slightly.

"No. We'll keep your names out of it for now, I promise. His house, have you called round there recently?"

Both women shook their heads. "We rarely go out. We both agreed it would be best if we stayed at home in case the children found their way home."

"What? You never go out?"

"Maybe when our husbands are at the house. Someone has to be there all the time. We even do our grocery shopping online now. I know how ridiculous that sounds, but we'd rather do that than miss our children if they showed up. We've heard of other kids escaping in similar circumstances."

"Okay, that's understandable. This is what we're going to do now: we'll take a drive over to your brother's house, see if he's at home, willing to speak to us. If he isn't there, then we'll issue an alert for him. Please, I'm asking you not to get in touch with him, no matter how tempted you might be. If you reached out to him or show your anger over the phone, you could be putting your children's lives in danger."

Both women gasped.

"We don't want to do that, you have our word," Jessica said, speaking for both of them.

"I'll leave you my card and promise that we'll be in touch soon, hopefully with good news."

Sara rose from the chair. Carla followed suit, and they both left the room with Jessica leading the way to the front door.

"I'm sorry. I should have spoken out about this earlier. Fiona has always had her suspicions, but I wasn't prepared to think badly of my brother. I realise how wrong I was now."

"Please don't feel bad. We don't know if your brother is guilty of anything yet. Speak soon. Try not to worry too much in the meantime."

"Easier said than done. Thank you for coming to see us, Inspector."

Sara and Carla jumped back in the car before either of them spoke.

"You think this is definitely to do with him?" Carla clipped her seat belt in place.

"Don't you? Right, here's what I think we should do. While I head over to Moore's address, I need you to contact all the parents, not just the ones we're due to see this evening. Ask them if they know a Chris or Christopher Moore. Let's get that pinned down first."

Sara drove. However, she found herself a little distracted, listening to Carla calling the parents.

"Nothing so far. Two more to ring."

"Stick with it."

Sara parked up behind a car at the top of Spinacre road. Carla hit the speaker button, and Stuart Wisdom's voice filled the car. Sara kept quiet, letting Carla ask the questions.

"Mr Wisdom, sorry to disturb you this evening, but we need to know if you've ever heard of a man called Christopher Moore."

Without hesitation Stuart said, "Yes. Chris used to work for me. I had to lay him off last month. Why?"

Carla punched the air. Sara made a sign to wind things up quickly. Carla cleared her throat and said, "It's a name that has cropped up through our enquiries. We'll have more information soon, sir. Enjoy the rest of your evening."

"Huh! You ring up and ask me if I know someone and refuse to divulge why? Has he got my daughter?"

"We don't know that, sir. My boss will be in touch with you tomorrow." Carla jabbed her finger at the phone to end the call.

"Shit! I hope he doesn't come over here. I know I would if I were in his situation. All right, we can't worry about that side of things now. Let's pay Chris a visit."

Sara started up the car and parked outside number thirty-three. They left the car and pushed open the clapped-out wooden gate. The concrete path had severe, almost dangerous cracks, and the front garden was overgrown even at this time of year. There was a light on in the hall.

"Looks like someone is home." Sara pressed the bell. It didn't respond to her touch, so she banged on the front door instead.

There was still no response. "I'm going to take a gander round the back."

Carla shuffled her feet nervously. "Okay, I'll stay here."

"Problem?"

Carla lowered her voice. "I don't think we should separate, it's too dangerous."

"All right. Come with me. We'll check all the windows at the side of the house."

"We should have asked his sisters what car he drives."

"Can you give one of them a call now?"

Carla rang Jessica from the side of the house. "Jessica, we're at your brother's address. We forgot to ask what car he drives…Okay, thanks for that. Be in touch again soon."

"So?"

"A Nissan Juke. She didn't know the reg number, only that it was a red one."

Sara searched the length of the road. "I can't see one."

"Maybe there's a garage around the back."

They continued to weave their way around the side of the house to the back garden that was equally overgrown and full of rubbish, including an old sofa and a stained mattress in the corner. "No garage out here. He might be using someone else's, perhaps renting one off a neighbour."

"Maybe."

Sara moved through the garden and peered in the kitchen window which was dimly lit by the light in the hall. There was no sign of life. "Damn. Looks like he's out."

Carla tutted. "The obligatory safety light on in the hall to deter possible burglars?"

"I'm guessing you're right. Okay, let's call it a day and head back to the station."

"What about the other parents?"

"I think they'll be a waste of time. My guess is that Chris Moore is the key to all this. Ring the parents to cancel the meetings."

They dropped back in the car and pulled away from the house. Sara carried out a three-point turn at the end of the road and headed back into the city, disappointment gushing through her veins.

"Shit! It was all going so well. Still, we've got more now than we had when we started our shift this morning. Mustn't get too disheartened."

"You think he's definitely behind this? Where's he keeping the kids?"

"Yes to your first question, and fuck knows to your second. If he's not here, maybe he's with them now, feeding them, possibly. I'm trying to be positive here, convincing myself the kids are still alive as no bodies have been recovered to date."

"You could be right. So bloody near and yet..."

"I know. Keep the faith, Carla. I feel it's only a matter of time before we catch the bastard, hopefully in the act."

"One thing that's bugging me."

"What's that?"

"Where does the woman fit into this?"

"There's still a lot for us to sort out yet. Is he connected to the mopeds? He has to be—it would appear he abducted Siobhan, right? If that's the case, where are the mopeds, the woman, the other men involved and the van? Once those things slot into place, we should be able to nail the bastard."

"Are you forgetting about the woman and the van? Craig and Will are on surveillance over there now."

Sara slammed the heel of her hand into her forehead. "Shit! It slipped my mind for a second. Okay, maybe that's where they're keeping the kids then. Do me a favour. Ring Will and ask if there's a red Juke sitting outside the house."

Carla rang her colleague, but his response was a negative one.

"Let's get back to the station and go over things. Our hands are tied without that warrant in place. I'll ring the DCI when we get back and ask her to put in a good word for us—or put a rocket up their arses, I should say."

Carla sniggered.

HE HAPPENED to be looking out of the window when he spotted the two women getting out of the car. He didn't recognise them so went into survival mode, switching off all the lights bar the one in the hallway, the one visible from the road. Then he'd flung himself on the two kids on the bed, placing a hand over each of their mouths, and waited, sweat pouring off his brow and dripping down his face and neck.

What the fuck? What were they doing here? How the hell has anything we've done brought them searching for me?

Two suggestions thrashed about his mind—his sisters had blabbed, putting two and two together finally, or Fran and Mick's latest abduction had led the police to his door.

Thank Christ I always park the Juke in the next road, just in case anything like this crops up. They'll be back, though, with a frigging warrant. That'll take time to obtain. All we need is another twenty-four hours and we'll be out of here.

CHAPTER 12

SARA PULLED the team off surveillance to go over things one more time. While she awaited Will and Craig's arrival, she rang DCI Price. "Sorry to bother you at home, ma'am. The truth is, I could do with your help in obtaining two warrants for two different addresses."

"You better fill me in."

Sara did just that. "My take is that something major is afoot. Things have been escalating all week."

"Okay, is there any chance these people know you could be onto them?"

Sara shook her head as if the DCI was in the room with her. Realising she wasn't, she said, "No, we've been careful up until now. The only thing that could have triggered a touch of doubt was if Chris Moore had been at home tonight. He wasn't."

"Where do you think he was?"

"Haven't got a clue. We know he wasn't with the other two as they were under surveillance. He could've been anywhere. At the other location, where they're possibly keeping the kids? Maybe. We just don't know. That's why it's imperative we get our hands on those warrants soon."

"Leave it with me, I'll see if I can pull a few strings. Are you going to call it a day now?"

"I'm going to go over things one last time with the team, see if we've missed anything, then yes, we're going to head home. Unless you want us to keep the two addresses under surveillance overnight?"

"I don't think that's necessary. Get some rest."

"I'll be in as usual in the morning. I only sit at home twiddling my thumbs anyway. Might as well come in and pace the floor around here while we wait for the warrants to arrive."

"I knew you wouldn't hack changing shifts for long. I'd suggest keeping half the team on the normal shift and half on the later shift if you sense something big is about to go down. Trust your instincts, Sara, they've always been spot on in the past."

"I will. Thanks, boss. Sorry to interrupt your evening."

"You haven't. I'll make the call now. See you tomorrow."

Sara left the office and relayed the information and the chief's suggestion to split the team up into different shifts. Between them, the team sorted that out swiftly.

"Right, I think we should go home now. I'm going to arrange with the desk sergeant for uniform to patrol the two properties every few hours. Now go, we'll run through everything we have in the morning," she told the team, her shoulders sagging as weariness set in.

Her colleagues drifted off, leaving Carla and Sara to switch off the computers and lights. They walked out of the station together.

"Are you going to be all right? Going home by yourself?"

"I'll have to be. I feel safer in the knowledge that Ted and Mavis are watching over the property during the day, plus I have a spy camera over the front door now acting as a deterrent. Don't fret about me, enjoy the rest of your evening. I'm coming in at nine tomorrow. I know I have you down for the later shift, and I'd like you to stick with that, whether Andrew is away or not. You need your time off."

Carla sighed heavily. "So do you. All right, I'll do it if it means you won't nag me."

Sara laughed and placed a hand over her chest. "Me, nag? Never."

They parted and followed each other out of the car park but went their separate ways at the first set of traffic lights. Sara's heart raced as she drove home, increasing in tempo the closer she got to the house. She had intentionally left the outside light on. Ted was walking past with Muffin when she locked up the car.

"We've been keeping an eye open for you, Sara."

She waved and smiled. "You're very kind, thanks, Ted."

Sara entered through the front door to be greeted by Misty. She swooped down to pick her fluffball up and snuggled into her fur. "Have you had a good day, munchkin?"

Misty rubbed her head around her chin. Sara slipped off her coat and shoes, juggling her cat in her arms as she did so, and walked through to the kitchen. She looked in the fridge at the lack of ingredients lurking there and opted to knock up a cheese and onion omelette, except she had no onions. "Oh well, a plain ol' cheese one will have to do. Let's feed you first, lovely."

After feeding Misty and whisking up a couple of eggs, she heated up the grill. Throwing the omelette mix in a pan, she sprinkled on the cheese she'd grated. Once the egg mixture looked cooked underneath, she placed the pan under the grill for the egg to puff up—a little trick her mother had taught her a few years ago.

Pleased with her effort, she took her dinner through to the lounge and switched on *Sky News*. Her mobile rang as she was finishing her meal. Her heart fluttered when Mark's name lit up the screen. "Hello, you. How's the course going?"

"It's boring. I used to really enjoy coming away to these things, not so much nowadays."

"Why? Because you've heard it all before?" She stretched her weary limbs out on the couch.

"No, well, yes, but the honest answer is that I'm missing you."

Sara's cheeks warmed. "You say the nicest things."

"It's the truth. You know what they say about distance and the heart, well, they're spot on, I'm telling you."

"If it's any consolation, I'm missing you, too—well, I am now I'm at home. I haven't had the chance during the day."

"Hectic day in other words, right?"

"And some. A couple more pieces of the puzzle slotted into place."

"How exciting. Does that mean you'll be making an arrest soon?"

"It does. Hopefully within the next day or two."

"*Yes*," he shouted.

She laughed, imagining him punching the air. "What are you doing tonight, apart from ringing me, of course?"

"Nothing much. A group of them have gone into town for a meal. I'm going to see what's on the room service menu. Exciting, eh?"

"You should have joined your colleagues."

"I'd rather sit here and talk to you instead."

Sara beamed. The more she spoke to Mark, the more she warmed to him. "Well, I've just had an omelette, nothing thrilling at this end."

"I can't wait for our meal out on Saturday. We're still on for that, right?"

"Of course. Why the doubt?" she asked, her brow forming a frown of uncertainty.

"No reason, apart from your busy schedule."

"You're worrying unnecessarily. It's only Thursday. Forty-eight hours to go yet."

"Actually, it's forty-six, but who's counting."

She chuckled. "You're an idiot." A noise in the kitchen caught her attention, and she slipped off the couch to investigate. Going through to the kitchen, she gasped. A rock was lying in the middle of the floor with a note wrapped around it. She looked up and saw the small window to the side of the back door broken.

"What's wrong...Sara...tell me? You're worrying me now...what is it?"

She ran a hand over her face and approached the stone. She cradled the phone between her ear and her shoulder and searched a drawer for a glove. She picked up the stone and read the note.

You've been warned. The time is getting nearer for you to meet your maker.

SHE GASPED AGAIN and zoned out from the situation until Mark's pleading voice sounded in her ear.

"Please, Sara. Tell me what's going on. I'm worried about you."

"I'm fine. Just a slight accident. The cat knocked a vase on the floor. I stepped on a piece of glass. I need to go and clear it up. Don't worry about me, I'll be all right. Enjoy your course. I'll ring you tomorrow evening, okay?"

"Phew, is that all? I thought something major had happened. All right, I'll let you go and sort that out and speak tomorrow." He blew a kiss down the line which Sara forgot to return before she ended the call.

What the fuck? She spent the next five minutes clearing up every shard of glass in case her precious cat stepped on it. This was getting ludicrous. She'd need to get the stone over to forensics ASAP for a fingerprint match, not that she expected to find one. *Who the hell is doing this? Making these horrible threats? Why? To warn me off? Off of what?* "No...are they warning me to stay away from Mark, is that it?"

Sara knew she should report the incident, but all she could think about was repairing the damage, at least covering up the gap in the frame where the glass used to be. She opened the back door cautiously and unlocked the garage. Emptying the contents of a cardboard box, she took it back into the kitchen along with a hammer and some nails she had in her handy toolbox her father had given her when she'd moved into her new home. "Damn, I'll have to ring a glazing firm now. I wonder if Ted will oversee the work for me." She covered the gaping hole, picked up her keys and locked the back door.

Warily searching around her, she trotted across the road to her neighbours' house.

Ted welcomed her into the hallway. Mavis appeared soon after.

"Hello, love. What can we do for you?" Ted asked, his brow wrinkled in concern.

"Someone threw a stone through a small back window in the kitchen. I wondered if I rang a glazing firm if you'd stay in the house for me while they carried out the work. Thought I'd check with you first before I placed the call."

"What? That's terrible. You only have to ask. Make the appointment, and I'll be there. Mind you, that'll cost you a bomb. Why don't I do it for you?"

"Would you? Could you? Isn't it difficult?"

"No, not at all. If it's the small single glazed window you're referring to, it should be easy to fix. I'll get the measurements, nip down to B&Q, source the glass and get a bit of beading to keep it in place. None of this dealing with messy putty nowadays, love. I'll fetch my coat and shoes and come over."

"It is that window. Maybe that's why they chose that one, easier to break. You're a treasure. I hate to impose on you after going out of your way to be so kind to me already."

"Nonsense," Mavis said. "Let him do it, love. He likes to be useful. What an upsetting thing for you to have to deal with, and you, a police officer."

"I know, laughable, isn't it? I'm expected to protect the general public and yet I can't protect my own home. They must have seen the camera over the front door. Maybe it peed them off."

Mavis nodded and tutted. "More than likely. Can you report it at work?"

"I'm going to have to now. Too much has happened to let it go. Please don't worry about your safety, though, will you? It's my house they're targeting, so that tells me it's personal and nothing to do with the neighbourhood. Sickening as that may be."

"We didn't see anything; we've been keeping an eye out during the day. Sorry to have let you down."

Sara stepped forward and hugged Mavis. "Don't be silly, you haven't let me down."

"Right, let's go sort this out. I've got some board in the garage. I'll pick that up on the way out," Ted said, pulling on his Puffa jacket.

"I've put some card over it for now, won't that do?"

Ted raised an eyebrow. "Not if it pees down during the night as forecasted."

. . .

IT TOOK TED thirty minutes to replace the card and measure the window. He was reluctant to leave her alone and even offered her a bed in their spare room for the night. Sara declined and assured him she would be okay, sending him back to his house with her spare key and instructions to place Misty in the lounge while he carried out the repairs. She trusted her instincts telling her she would be safe the rest of the evening. If the other incidents were anything to go by, once the deed had been carried out, nothing else had happened in the hours that followed.

Surprisingly, she slept well that night and woke up at six the following morning. Rising from her bed, she trotted downstairs to check the board was still in place at the window, made herself a coffee and took it upstairs to get ready for work.

CHAPTER 13

WHEN SHE ARRIVED at the station at eight-thirty, she was taken aback to see the whole team sitting at their desks. "What in God's name are you all doing here?"

"We're so close, none of us wanted to miss out if an arrest was on the cards today," Carla told her, rising from her chair and heading for the vending machine. She returned and deposited the paper cup in Sara's hand.

"I'm flabbergasted. You guys truly are the best team to be surrounded by. Thank you, I mean that sincerely. You're the greatest." Unexpected tears welled up. She wiped them away with her sleeve and gestured for Carla to follow her into the office. She closed the door behind them and walked around the desk. Drink in hand, she sank into her chair and heaved out a long breath. "Something else happened last night." She opened the carrier bag she'd placed on the desk, popped on a glove and extracted the stone and the message, holding it out for Carla to read.

"What the actual fuck? You have to do something about this, Sara."

"I know. Let's get this case out of the way, and I'll do it then."

"No. You have to do something *now*. These are *death* threats. You're being foolish if you ignore them. And yes, I'm frigging concerned about your safety."

Sara popped the stone back in the bag and placed it on the floor by her desk. "Once the arrest has been made, I'll take the stone over to the lab to get it tested. There's no point worrying about it now. I need to concentrate solely on finding the children. I appreciate what you're saying, but let me deal with things my way, all right?"

Carla buried her head in her hands and growled. Dropping her hands into her lap, she said, "At times you're sooooo bloody annoying, you know that?"

Sara grinned. "I know. Look, my take on it is while these things are happening, I've not really felt threatened as such. I know that probably doesn't make sense to you, but it's true. I'd be more concerned if I shared my house with a partner. The fact is, I don't. I'm out all day so not likely to come into contact with the person or persons responsible."

"That's unbelievably warped. Were you out when the stone flew through your window? No, you were at home. What about when Mark's car was damaged? No, you were there. Jesus, Sara, it seems to me that I'm more worried about this shit than you are. Why?"

"Unless you've suffered the pain I've been through, it's hard for you to comprehend. Maybe I have a blasé attitude…I don't know. Just don't hate me for it. Let me deal with this my own way, okay?"

"All right, I hear you. You're still going to report it, aren't you?"

"Eventually. I'll get the stone checked out and see what comes back from the results."

Carla huffed out a complaint and left the room. Sara sipped her coffee and then tackled her post, keen to get it all out of the way before she and the team discussed the case and the plans they had to bring these bastards to justice.

THE REST of the day dragged by, their hands tied without the much-needed warrants. DCI Price chased the warrants a few times during the course of the day, her frustration as prominent as Sara's. Time was running out. Not hearing anything by five-thirty, Sara struck out at a chair, kicking it the length of the incident room. "What is wrong with them? All it takes is someone to look over the case and sign the bloody document. How frigging difficult is that?"

The team were aware it was a rhetorical question. At six-ten, Barry called across for Sara to join him.

"What's up?"

"I've got a hit on the van. An ANPR camera picked it up on the outskirts of the city."

"Shit. Keep your eye on it, Barry." Sara was in two minds whether to jump in the car to try to tail the van or stay put, waiting by the phone for the call to come in.

"I've lost it again."

"Where?" Sara asked, thumping her thigh.

"Not far from where I said I spotted it."

"Bollocks. We need that van, need to know what these guys are up to. Okay, I'm making the call. Fed up with sitting around here on my arse. Jill, are you all right to stay here and man the phones?"

"Yep, my Mum promised to stay over tonight. I had a feeling it was all going to kick off and knew I wanted to be part of it."

"That's great to hear. You stay here. The rest of you pair up. We're going to scout this city until we find the fuckers. Carla, get in touch with Jeff, ask him to get uniform to keep a lookout and report to us any sightings they have of the van."

"On it now." Carla picked up the phone.

Will and Barry teamed up, and Christine and Craig did the same.

Sara grabbed her coat and gave Jill the thumbs-up. "Ring us if that bloody warrant comes through."

"Right away, boss. Good luck."

The six team members raced down the stairs and out of the main entrance. Jeff also shouted 'good luck' as they rushed past him.

In the car, as she buckled up her seat belt, Sara asked, "Am I doing the right thing?"

"I think so. We'll soon find out," Carla replied.

The convoy set off in the direction of the last sighting of the van. They hadn't travelled far when the radio sparked into life.

"Get that, Carla, tell them we're en route and contact the others, tell them to head for the centre, too."

Shit! Two mopeds had been sighted in the pedestrian area of town. A uniformed officer had raised the alarm and shouted at the suspects. They'd thrown acid in his face. The bastards!

Her heart pounded heavily against her ribs. She had a sinking feeling they were going to be too late, again. "Not long now. Please, please be there."

"All units be on the lookout for two mopeds heading towards Tupsley. Dangerous men. Approach with caution. They must be caught." The controller's voice filled the car, adding to Sara's anxiety.

Adrenaline pumped through her system faster than a speeding jet, at one point making it difficult for her to breathe properly.

Carla placed a hand on her arm. "Are you all right?"

Sara nodded and swerved past a vehicle that had been brought to a sudden, abrupt stop in the road. She blasted her horn. "Fucking idiot. Get out of my way. Can't he bloody hear the siren?"

"He probably panicked, most people do when confronted with a siren, you know that. God, I hope we catch them soon."

Sara leant over the steering wheel. "Is that them? In front of us, look."

"I think it is."

"Hold tight. I'm gonna knock them off their bikes if I have to."

"Be careful. What if you're wrong and it turns out to not be them? You'll lose your job for using the vehicle as a battering ram."

"Who cares?"

Carla groaned. "You should. It's your livelihood we're talking about. Be careful," she warned a second time.

"Damn and blast. One of them darted down the alley. Get on the radio. Tell Barry and Will to chase him." She pressed down on the accelerator, and the car lunged forward.

Carla clung on to her seat with one hand while she spoke on the radio with the other.

No matter how fast Sara went, she suspected the moped rider, being much slower and seeing her gain on him, had something up his sleeve. She proved to be right when he turned left into the park where the van had picked up Lara Parker the day before. The bike went across the grass. Sara drove after him, but the ground was boggy, unsuitable for a car. She slammed the brakes on and thumped the steering wheel. "Shit. Get Craig to go round the long way, see if he can cut him off." Sara reversed the car, but the wheels spun in the mud; they were stuck. She flung open her car door and watched the moped rise up the hill and stop at the top. The driver gave her the finger, revved the bike a few times and continued on his journey, doing a rotation on his bike at the top, not dissimilar to a doughnut carried out by a successful rider once they've won a championship race.

She felt like breaking down and crying, but what use would that be? No, she needed to get the car out of this shit and on the road again. She was far from finished with him.

* * *

THE GANG MET up and were jubilant about how the evening had gone. They were two million quid richer. Time to divide the money and get out of there.

"That was a close one, man. So much for the bikes being slower, eh, Chris?" Tory prodded him as Chris counted the money and placed it in piles.

"You trying to deliberately mess things up? Hoping that your pile will end up bigger?" Chris laughed and continued counting.

Half an hour later, and the money was sorted. They all counted their share and bagged it up into their relative bags, broad grins on their faces.

"We did it, guys. We pulled it off. It was nice knowing you. Good luck in the future," Chris said.

Five mill, split four ways. I'm tempted to kill the others and take the whole pot. If only the police hadn't come knocking at my door...

CHAPTER 14

WHEN THE TEAM arrived back at the station, Sara was furious that between them, they'd managed to lose the damn bikes. Her anger intensified when Jill told her they were still waiting for the warrants to be granted.

"You're being too hard on us all," Carla pointed out. "Maybe that's why they chose to use bikes in the first place, ease of escape being at the top of the perps' list."

"You're probably right. I'm still bloody livid. To be that close only to see them ride off into the darkness. Okay, we need to stop dwelling on it now. Patrol cars are on alert. It's imperative we get those damn warrants ASAP. Don't these people know the meaning of the word *urgent*? Don't answer that, I'm venting my anger. Right, first things first. I need to ring the hospital, see if there's any news on our colleague who was attacked."

Ten minutes later, Sara had her answer. Wayne Durrant had suffered ninety percent burns to his face. He would be treated with the same care and dignity as Angela Guppy. Sara's heart went out to the young officer and his family. He'd only been married for two years and had a six-month-old baby. Life sucked at times.

Sara rejoined the rest of the team. "Right, let's forget about the mopeds for now. What do we know about the van, anything?"

"It's not been seen since our last sighting. Either they've dumped it or they've covered up the number plate," Barry suggested.

"Either way, that's put the kibosh on things for us."

The team bounced ideas around for the next few hours until finally, dead on her feet, Sara ordered them to go home.

"We'll start with clear heads in the morning. Thanks for all your efforts today, chaps and chapesses. I know it's Saturday tomorrow, but we're so close."

When Sara got home, she immediately went through to the kitchen to inspect Ted's handiwork and was amazed at how well it had turned out. It was almost two a.m., far too late to go over and thank the kind man in person. She'd have to do it in the morning either before she set off for work or over the phone when she arrived.

Misty was circling her legs for attention. Sara fed her and let her out to go to the toilet, then together they climbed the stairs. Sara managed to strip off and fall into bed before her eyes drooped. She was asleep within seconds of her head hitting the pillow.

SARA SLEPT RIGHT through the night, and when the alarm went off at seven the next morning, she was tempted to knock it on the floor and go back to sleep. She didn't. Thirty minutes later, she was outside getting ready to jump in her car. She glanced over at Ted and Mavis's house. There was a light on in the front room. She knocked gently on the door in case only one of them was up. Ted opened the door wearing a huge smile.

"Sorry I didn't come over and show my appreciation last night, Ted. I didn't get in until around two. It looks fabulous. How much do I owe you?"

"Long day for you and up early again this morning. You watch you don't burn yourself out, love. Just pay for the materials, fifty-nine pounds. Later will do, you don't have to worry about it now."

"No, I can't do that. What about the time it took you to fix it? You know how much it would have cost if I'd called a professional out, Ted."

"I know. It didn't take me long. Go, we'll chat later. It was my pleasure."

Sara smiled and placed a kiss on his cheek. "I'm a bugger for not keeping cash on me. I'll stop off at the bank and get the money today, settle up with you this evening then, if that's all right?"

"It is. Now shoo."

"You're a guardian angel in disguise, that's what you are, dear man. I can't thank you enough for looking after me like this."

His eyes watered, and Sara imagined he was thinking about the daughter he'd lost recently.

"You're welcome. You're a lovely lass, Sara. If I can be of help in the future, let me know."

"Thank you. You'll probably regret saying that one day." She smiled again and turned to walk away.

"Never. Be safe out there."

Standing alongside the car, she waved and shouted, "I will." Sliding behind the steering wheel, she pulled out of her road and hit the country lane that led into the city. Her mind was full of different scenarios of how her day would progress once she arrived at work. Top priority had to be to get DCI Price to chase up those damn warrants.

As it happened, DCI Price drove into her parking slot in front of her at the station. "Hello there. Don't ask what I'm doing in on a Saturday and I won't do the same. How's it going? I take it the warrants came through after I left yesterday."

Sara shook her head and pressed the key fob to lock her car. "Nope. It's getting beyond a joke, ma'am. I was going to come and see you first thing, ask you if you wouldn't mind giving them a virtual boot up the backside."

DCI Price's lips pulled into the straightest of lines. "It would be my pleasure. Jesus, how do they expect us to do our jobs with their lax attitude? I'll get on it now, be in touch with you after I've blasted them, how's that?"

They walked through the main entrance and up the stairs together. "That would be brilliant."

They parted at the top of the stairs. Sara entered the incident room to find Carla, Jill, Craig and Christine, all at their desks. Will and Barry walked in behind her.

"You lot are great, that's all. The chief is chasing the warrants now. I'll nip into my office, see what crap is awaiting me there, and I'll be with you in a jiffy. Yes, Carla, a coffee would be wonderful."

She'd just made it to her chair when her landline rang. "The warrants will be with you within the hour, DI Ramsey."

Sara let out a relieved sigh. "Thank you, ma'am. Your intervention is greatly appreciated. Let's hope we can nail these bastards today."

"I've just heard about the moped incident. Shocking they should use acid again."

"We don't have any evidence linking the crimes apart from what happened to Siobhan and her mother, but I'm willing to put my neck on the line and say they are linked and we're dealing with the same gang."

"I'm inclined to agree with you. Keep me informed."

"I will, ma'am. Thank you." Sara hung up and punched the air as Carla entered the room and placed a steaming cup in front of her.

"Good news?"

"If it comes to fruition, yes. The warrants should be in our grubby little hands within the hour. That gives me ten minutes dealing with this shit, and then we'll formulate yet another plan. This time I'm determined to pounce on these bastards."

"I'll let the others know."

"Everything all right? You seem a little down this morning." Sara pointed to the chair opposite.

Carla shook her head and left the room without saying a word.

Crap! What's going on there? So unusual for her not to be smiley.

Sara got cracking on her paperwork and left her desk ten minutes later. She joined the others in the incident room. Casting a concerned eye in Carla's direction, she crossed the room to speak with her. "Are you all right?"

"Fine. I'd rather not talk about it now. I'll tell you when these bastards are banged up in a cell."

"If that's what you want?"

"It is." Carla smiled, but Sara noted the pain swimming in her eyes.

Had she missed the signs? Had her partner been suffering over the past few days and she'd been so wrapped up in her own problems that she'd failed to notice? She didn't think so. No, this was something new. Something she was desperate to get to the bottom of when they had some spare time on their hands.

"Right, let's get a plan of action organised, ready for when we get the all-clear to advance. We need to hit both addresses at the same time. Jill, you stay here and man the phones. Marissa, welcome back from your holiday. Spend the next half an hour getting up to speed on the case if you will."

"Already done that, boss. I'm raring to go," the chubby constable told her, her white teeth glowing against the tanned skin she'd obtained from her time chilling out on a beach in Spain.

"Great. Marissa, Barry, Craig and Christine, why don't you take the Grangers' house? Will, you, Carla and I will hit Chris Moore's place. We need to bear in mind that the suspects are likely to be dangerous. Watch out for any form of acid at the premises. We've got a couple of Taser-trained folks amongst us, yes?"

Barry and Christine both raised their hands, as did Carla.

"Okay, that's two on each team. Also, we need to be aware that there could be children at the premises. If they're not there, we need to find evidence of where they're being kept. That's vitally important, you all know that."

The phone rang on Carla's desk. Answering it, Carla grinned from ear to ear and replaced the phone. "We've got the warrants."

"Excellent news. Let's hit the road."

The room was filled with the noise of scraping chairs and excited chatter. The phone on Carla's desk rang again. Carla raised her hand. Sara clicked her fingers, instructing the team to quieten down.

Carla ended the call. "Two mopeds have shown up on the edge of the River Wye."

Sara sighed. "Could be a coincidence. Unlikely, but…Okay, let's not let this distract us. We'll let SOCO deal with that while we go pick up the suspects."

SARA PULLED up outside Chris Moore's house. His car wasn't there. "Shit, same situation as before. Will, how's that shoulder of yours? We're going to have to break the door down if necessary. I'm not leaving here until I've seen what's inside."

"Dodgy, boss. But I'll kick it, no problem."

"Good man, let's go."

They all left the car and made their way up the path to the house. Sara's mobile rang. She took a few steps back to answer it.

"Barry, what's up?"

"We're at the location, boss. No van in sight. Do you still want us to enter the property?"

"Damn! Yep, do that. Gather any evidence you can. Also have a chat with the neighbours, ask when they last saw the Grangers. We've got the same thing here. I'm going to ring the station, get an alert put out on both vehicles. Ring me with your findings. Good luck."

"You, too, boss."

Sara ended the call and rejoined Carla and Will. "Do your thing, Will."

He nodded and kicked out a panel in the old wooden door with relative ease. He poked his arm through the hole and reached up to open the door from the inside. Sara patted him on the shoulder when he stood next to her. Tasers at the ready, Carla and Sara took the lead and entered the house. Going from room to room, there was evidence that children had been kept there in the form of bowls and plastic tumblers draining in the kitchen. In the lounge there was a bed. On top, poking out of the sheet, were a couple of dolls.

"Shit, we couldn't make anything out in this room when we were here the other day and looked through the window."

Carla nodded. "Don't dwell on it. Want to check upstairs?"

"Too right."

The three of them ascended the creaky staircase slowly and searched all the rooms. No sign of life in any of them. In the main bedroom they found the wardrobe door open. Sara inched forward and peered through the door, gasping when she saw what lay ahead of her.

"Damn, it's a secret room."

Carla peered over her shoulder. "Fuck. How many kids did they have, and where are they now? Have we spooked them?"

Sara growled. "It bloody looks that way. All right, back up. Let's keep it clean for SOCO to do their thing. I'm going to ring the others. Put some gloves on, guys, we need to start looking through drawers et cetera. We need to know where these kids have gone. Evidence of another address, something along those lines would help."

Sara and Carla backed out of the room.

Sara rang Barry at the other house. "Anything?"

"Not so far, boss. No sign of any kids being held here."

"Okay, we think they were kept here. We've got a false room kitted out with beds. No sign of life here. Search for any form of paperwork, Barry. Look for passports, anything along those lines. Shit, I'm going to get on to Jill to warn the ports and airports. If these guys are running, that's where they'll likely be heading."

"I agree. We'll search high and low if necessary, boss."

Sara ended the call and rang Jill. "Jill, here's where we are." She explained the situation at both residences and then ordered, "I need you to make the ports and the airports aware. We have to assume they'll be travelling under their own names. It's all we've got to go on right now."

"What if they're staying in this country, boss?"

"I've got an alert out for both vehicles, that's all angles covered as far as I'm aware. I'm going to ring SOCO now. Speak later." Sara immediately rang the SOCO department and gave them the address of both residences with instructions of what she needed.

The next couple of hours zoomed past. Barry rang a couple of times during their stay at the house to keep her up to date on what evidence they had found. It wasn't until everyone had reconvened at the station that an important call came in that got them all excited.

Carla took the call. "That's brilliant. We'll try and get some bodies up there. Can you delay the ferry for an hour or two? I know that's asking a lot. Okay, that's understandable. Get some officers on board the ferry ready to swoop then if you would."

Sara was eager to know and urged Carla to divulge what she'd heard the second she hung up.

"ANPR cameras picked up the van heading towards Liverpool. The van was then spotted in the queue by one of the port officials. Looks like they're en route from Birkenhead to Belfast."

"That's feasible. Will and Craig, get on the road. Haul their arses back down here."

The two men rushed out of the incident room.

Sara's heart raced so fast she thought the darn thing was going to give up on her. "One down, one more to go. I have a good feeling about this, peeps. Might be that I'm dying for a pee, though. I should remedy that before I deposit a puddle."

The team's laughter followed her out of the incident room and into the toilet. After relieving herself, she studied her reflection in the mirror. "You're looking old, girl. Time for some relaxation after this case is over, methinks."

It was another few hours of pacing the office before they heard from Will and Craig. They'd boarded the ferry in search of the couple and managed to delay the ferry's departure for half an hour. A little girl shouted at a uniformed officer helping them to conduct the search. She cried out her name and that she wanted her mummy, adding that the nasty people had stolen her. Fran and Mick Granger were arrested on the spot and the child handed over to Will and Craig.

Relief flooded through Sara. She rang Stuart Wisdom. "Stuart, it's DI Sara Ramsey. Are you sitting down?"

"I am now. Don't keep me waiting. Have you found her body?"

"No. We've found her alive and well. She's coming home, Stuart, as fast as my men can get her to you. She's coming home." Tears sprang to her eyes as the words caught in her throat. This was the better side of the job, reuniting loved ones, especially when everything was stacked against them.

"Oh my God. Thank you, thank you. When can I see her?"

"Soon. My men are bringing her back from Liverpool right now. They should arrive in a couple of hours. We'll need to get her checked out at the hospital. Why don't you come to the station and be here when she arrives? She'll need a relative and a friendly face beside her for what she's about to go through."

"I don't care what you put her through if it helps to bang the bastards up. Jesus, this is surreal. I never thought I'd receive a call from you to say she was alive. Thank you, Inspector, even that doesn't sound enough."

"I know. It was our pleasure, sir."

Feeling elated and a little emotional, Sara bought the team a coffee. "Let's stick with it, guys. Find Chris, wherever he's hiding."

Another hour dragged past, then all hell let loose.

"Boss," Christine shouted to gain her attention.

Sara marched across the room. "What is it?"

"There's a police chase going on along the M4. They're in pursuit of Chris Moore's car."

"Hallelujah! Fingers crossed they stop him, guys. I bet the fucker was en route to Heathrow. Jill, can you check for me, see if he's booked on a flight?"

Jill rang the airport and received the answer within ten minutes. "Yep, a flight to Mexico. I've made them aware of the situation, and they've assured me that if he manages to escape our guys on the motorway, he'll be arrested before he boards the plane."

"Excellent. How's the pursuit going, Christine?"

"Last I heard, they've managed to get him off the motorway. They're organising the stingers now."

"Good. We're that close." She held up her forefinger and thumb with an inch gap in between.

"Actioned. He tried to run, but two officers jumped him."

The team congratulated each other on a job well done, and Sara danced her way up the corridor to tell the chief.

DCI Price was equally elated when Sara shared the news. "What a triumph that is. You should be super pleased with yourself, Sara."

"Teamwork, boss. You played your part by getting the warrants for us. If you hadn't intervened, well, the three of them would have been in different countries by now, and you know the consequences of that."

"I do. Now comes the hard part, right? Getting the truth out of them. Any plans on how you propose doing that?"

"I thought I'd work on the woman first. Go from there. Sometimes they're easier to break down, although that's not always the case."

"I'm sure you'll accomplish it somehow. Let me know if you need me to sit in on any interviews to give you extra clout."

"I will. Right, I better get back to it. I have dozens of questions I need to jot down before the suspects arrive."

"Good luck."

Sara left the room and was walking up the corridor when she noticed Carla enter the ladies' toilet with her head down. Sara pushed the door open and waited for her to come out of the cubicle. If her ears weren't deceiving her, it sounded like Carla was crying. The toilet flushed, and a red-eyed Carla opened the cubicle door. She was shocked to see Sara standing there.

"Hey, what's with the tears, love?"

Carla waved her concerns away. "Nothing. Needed a release, sorry. You have enough on your mind at the moment. My problems can wait."

Sara waited for Carla to step out of the cubicle and then approached her. She placed a hand on each of her partner's arms. "No, they can't. I'm a good listener if you want to give it a shot. Is this a personal matter?"

Carla nodded. "Leave it for now. We have suspects to question."

"In a few hours. Come on, Carla, spill. I promise not to judge."

"I know you won't. All right..." She sniffled and wiped her nose on a piece of toilet paper. "Andrew has finished with me."

Sara's eyes widened. "What? I thought you guys were solid. Weren't you discussing getting engaged?"

"So did I. Yep, we've been discussing it for months, but nothing has come of it. I know why now."

"Did he give a reason?"

"He's met someone else. The thing that has hurt the most is that he admitted he started seeing her not long after he moved in with me."

"The effing slimeball!" Sara pulled Carla into her arms as the tears flowed again. "I'm sorry, love. Some men just aren't worth it, are they? They don't realise they're onto a good thing until it's too late. He'll regret his actions one day, you can be sure of that."

Carla stepped away and dried her eyes. "The thing is, I've missed my period. It was due last week."

Sara ran a hand through her hair. "Jesus, are you usually regular?"

"As clockwork. What am I going to do now?"

"What do you want to do? Keep it? Of course, I might be jumping the gun by asking that question. You should leave it a few weeks. Maybe working on this case has messed up your cycle."

"I'd call that clutching at straws myself."

"Possibly. Do you want kids?"

"I've never really thought about it. I suppose in the future, not at this time in my life, and especially when my fella has just dumped me. Jesus, Mum is going to go berserk."

"Let's wait a while before you tell your mum. You need to buy a test. That's always a good indication, although sometimes they can give a false reading. Oh, babe, I feel for you and the decisions you have ahead of you."

"Thanks. I'm sorry to put a dampener on the celebrations. I couldn't hold it back any longer."

"Don't be silly. I'm gutted you felt you couldn't share this with me sooner."

"It wasn't intentional. I had to get it sorted in my own mind first. It has been difficult to come to terms with."

"I hear you. Come on, dry your eyes, I'll treat you to a coffee. That'll help chase the blues away. Promise me you'll buy one of those tests over the weekend and ring me with the result straight away." Sara deliberately avoided saying the P word.

"I promise. I'll try and push this aside. I've managed to do it for a few days. I suppose the relief of capturing the suspects and finding Siobhan alive stirred up emotions in me that I never knew existed."

"Understandable. I feel the same, if I'm honest with you."

"Thanks for listening, Sara."

"Hey, we're a team. I'm always here for you, you know that. Try not to worry too much."

"I promise. Let's go nail these bastards for what they've done to those kiddies. It's a shame we haven't found out where the kids are yet."

"That's the worrying part for me."

When they entered the incident room, Barry waved to gain their attention. "I've got it."

Sara and Carla rushed over to his desk. "Got what?"

He pointed at the small black notebook on his desk. "Where the kids are."

Sara's heart hammered. "You're not winding me up, are you?"

"No, I promise, boss. We found the book at the Grangers' house. They've all left the country, but I have the addresses where they're now living."

"That's amazing news. I'm going to pass this info on to the DCI, let her deal with that side of things. It's above my pay grade. Wow! I can't believe it."

Barry handed her the notebook. Sara rushed back up the corridor, barging into a couple of officers. "Sorry, chaps, urgent matter."

"Always in a rush, DI Ramsey," one of them shouted back.

"I am when kiddies' lives are at risk."

"We'll forgive you in that case."

Sara charged into DCI Price's office without knocking. Gasping for breath, she placed the notebook on the desk in front of her. "The kids. That's where they've been dispatched to. We need to get them back, boss."

DCI Price fell back in her chair, taking the notebook with her.

"Fuck, that's all we need. Okay, leave this with me, I'll put the wheels in motion. Congratulate the team for me. You've all gone above and beyond on this one."

"Haven't we? I never thought we'd find them."

"Don't contact the parents yet. Let's bide our time on that. I'd hate to get the parents' hopes up."

"I agree. A few more days won't make a difference."

A COUPLE of hours passed before the first suspect arrived. Sara and Carla walked down the stairs together, strength in numbers and all that. The minute she laid eyes on Chris Moore, she detested him and everything he stood for. He glared at her, probably pissed off that she and her team had scuppered his plans to flee the country.

"Welcome, Mr Moore, nice of you to join us. We'll get you settled in your cell first before we interview you. Just to let you know that we've also captured your associates. Fran and Mick Granger are on their way down from Liverpool now. They should be here any second, in fact."

There was a glint in his eye where she expected to find hatred or anger at the very least. However, Moore refused to say anything. The desk sergeant escorted him to the cell and returned to his desk as the front door opened and in walked Will and Craig with the other two suspects.

"Well done, boys. I'd like to question Mrs Granger first. Take her through to Interview Room One please and place her husband in a cell next to Chris Moore's."

The husband and wife glanced at each other, another weird look that was hard to decipher.

Sara turned up the passageway with Carla. "Did you notice anything?"

"Not really. What?"

"I don't know. My take is we haven't got all the gang members yet." Sara recapped the CCTV footage and tried to match it to the frames of the men they had in custody. "There's no way either Mick or Fran were on the bikes, their physiques don't match. Yes, for Chris Moore, but I think we're missing another body. We need to worm that information out of them."

"Put a plea bargain on the table perhaps."

Sara nodded. "Let's see how we go for now. Fran seems fraught to me, as if she'll spill the beans if we push her enough."

"Go for it. Hit her hard from the get-go, if that's what it'll take."

They entered the room and sat at the desk. Carla prepared the recording machine while they waited for Fran Granger to join them. Will brought the woman in a few minutes later accompanied by the duty solicitor.

"Would you like a drink?" Sara asked.

"Tea please," Granger replied quietly.

The solicitor shook her head. They both sat opposite Carla and Sara. Granger bowed her head in shame.

"Can you get that for me, Will? Thanks." When Will returned with the drinks and left the room again, Carla started the recording and said the usual verbiage into the machine. "You've heard the charges against you. What do you have to say for yourself, Fran?"

She glanced sideways at her solicitor rather than reply.

The solicitor whispered something in her client's ear and then smiled at Sara. "My client will tell you everything, only if there is some form of bargain on the table."

"We're always willing to negotiate providing the information is good enough. I'd need to run it past the CPS first. Give me two seconds." Sara left the room and rang her contact at the Crown Prosecution Service who agreed to a deal if the information provided led to further arrests. Sara returned to the room. "You've got your deal. I suspect there are other gang members involved. If you can provide us with names, then yes, a deal is on the table."

Fran Granger immediately sat back in her chair and revealed everything, including the name of the fourth member of the gang and how they'd originally met through an online site called Revenge Matters.

"Are you telling me that all this was about revenge?"

Granger nodded.

"For the recording, Mrs Granger."

"Yes," she replied. "Each of the kids belongs to someone who the gang members wanted to get revenge on."

Sara felt sick to her stomach. "Why? Why take it out on the kids?"

"It was something Tory and Chris came up with. Mick and I went along with it to keep the peace. All we wanted was to get some money behind us at the end of the day, to start afresh in Ireland."

"With a stolen kid to join you, right?" Sara added.

"She wasn't part of the plan. The others will tell you how much I hate kids, but I was drawn to her, she was different. She shouldn't have seen her mother killed like that. I felt sorry for her. Her pain tugged at my heart."

"I see. Until then, you didn't think you had one, right?"

Granger glared at Sara. "I knew I had a heart, but that child, well, she'd been through enough in her young life. Mick and I thought we'd be able to ease her pain by giving her a good home."

"She already had a good home. If you felt that strongly about it, why didn't you give her back to her father?"

Her chin dropped onto her chest again. "My need was greater."

Sara clenched and unclenched her fists a few times in an attempt to control her temper. The interview lasted about an hour after that. She had everything she needed—times, places, motives. Now, what remained to be done was to put out an alert to find Tory Broad.

The rest of the day consisted of Sara interviewing the two men they had in custody. Mick proved to be as willing as his wife and also demanded a plea bargain. Sara granted him one as she was convinced the married couple weren't the brains behind the plan, even though they had a hand in abducting the children. They cared for the kids, whereas the other two members of the gang, Tory and Chris, were the ones mainly behind the plan and the outcome, including the two murders and the acid attacks.

By five o'clock that evening, they had all four members sitting in a cell and the two million the gang had split, deposited in the evidence room safe.

The team finished off the shift by going for a quick drink at the Red Bull down the road before Sara said farewell and drove home. As her journey came to an end, a griping sensation filled her stomach. She had no idea what lay ahead of her. She exhaled a sigh of relief when she entered her home to find everything as it should be.

EPILOGUE

SHE THOUGHT over what would need to be done on Monday while she got ready for her date with Mark. The necessary paperwork would need to be filled out. The suspects had already been formerly charged and would be shipped out to the remand centre sometime during the day on Monday. The charges thrown at them ranged from kidnapping to murder with a few ABH charges thrown into the mix for good measure.

Sara dressed in a mid-calf black dress and pulled her best coat out of the wardrobe. Mark picked her up at six forty-five and whistled, impressed by her appearance as he held the car door open for her. Her cheeks flared up. It had been a while since a man had complimented her in such a way.

Over their sumptuous meal at the atmospheric restaurant, they shared the news of how their week had panned out. Sara left out the part about the paint being daubed on her front door and the fact her window had been smashed, thinking it might put Mark off her. She liked him, and she was beginning to care about him. He told her about some of the light-hearted moments that had happened during his course, along with all the serious stuff he'd dealt with.

By the end of the evening, a few bevvies too many drunk, they left

Mark's car in town and caught a taxi home. Sara insisted Mark should stay the night, this time in her bed.

They spent the following morning in bed. She rang her mother around eleven to tell her she was on the way and asked if she could bring a plus-one for Sunday lunch. In spite of her nerves, Sara was delighted when her family accepted Mark with warmth and kindness.

When they left her parents' house, Sara dropped Mark back into town to pick up his car. There they parted as Mark was eager to go home and get ready for what work had to throw at him on Monday. Sara agreed, although she missed him like crazy when she returned to her home alone.

During her evening cuddle with Misty, she received one of two phone calls. The first was from Carla. "Hi, just thought I'd share the good news with you...I'm not pregnant!" her partner shouted, the relief in her voice evident.

"I'm thrilled for you, love. Go you. Any news from Andrew?"

"Yep, he called round this morning to collect his gear. I was tempted to attack his clothes with a pair of scissors before he got here, but I restrained myself."

"Good on ya. He's not worth it. You'll find someone better, mark my words."

"You sound happy. Have you had a good weekend?"

"I am, and yes, hardly the weekend off, but the best day off I've had in a long time. I'll fill you in tomorrow."

"Bloody tease."

"Aren't I? Enjoy the rest of your evening, Carla, I'm going to relax in a bubble bath now."

"Sounds wonderful. See you tomorrow."

Sara ended the call and dislodged Misty from her lap to run the bath. She took her mobile with her. As she sank into the bubbles, the second call arrived. She was tempted to ignore the ringing telephone, but her inquisitive nature got the better of her. "Hello."

"Sara Ramsey?"

"Yes, who's this?" She sat up, alert, the water almost slopping out of the bath in her haste.

"A voice from the past. DI James Smart."

Sara closed her eyes. She'd dreaded receiving a call from this man. "What can I do for you, James?"

"There's been a development in your husband's case that I wanted you to be aware of."

Her mouth dried up, and she cleared her throat. "What's that? Have you caught the bastard who shot him?"

"We believe so. You're aware that he was part of a gang, right?"

"Yes, of course. Please, don't draw this out any longer than necessary, just tell me why you're ringing me."

"Sorry. Nothing might come of it, but I thought I'd better warn you anyway."

"Come of what? His arrest?"

"Yes. In our experience, once a gang leader has been arrested, the rest of the gang do everything in their power to antagonise the victim's family. I wanted to warn you, that's all."

She swallowed down the gasp that was dying to erupt. "Thanks for the warning. I'll put all the necessary security in place." She ended the call and flopped back in the bath. "Your call has come too late, buster. Their revenge has already begun."

THE END

LETTER TO THE READER

Dear Reader,

Well that was a heart-in-the-mouth read. Sara did exceptional work tracking down the culprits before they managed to escape to foreign shores, as well as facing everything else thrown at her in her personal life.

But there are more crimes to solve. The next case is a perplexing one when the body of an unidentified woman turns up in a hotel room.

The secrets revealed after her death shock the community.

Find out what lies in store for Sara both professionally and personally in the next instalment by downloading a copy of The Dead Can't Speak Here

Thank you for choosing to read my work.

M. A. Comley

P.S. Reviews are wondrous gifts for authors and prompt them to keep writing even when the temptation strikes to give up, won't you consider leaving one today?

KEEP IN TOUCH WITH THE AUTHOR

Sign up to M A Comley's newsletter for announcements regarding new releases and special offers.
http://smarturl.it/8jtcvv

Or follow on:
Twitter
https://twitter.com/Melcom1
Blog
http://melcomley.blogspot.com
Facebook
http://smarturl.it/sps7jh
BookBub
www.bookbub.com/authors/m-a-comley

ABOUT THE AUTHOR

M A Comley is a New York Times and USA Today bestselling author of crime fiction. To date (Feb 2018) she has over 82 titles published.

Her books have reached the top of the charts on all platforms in ebook format, Top 20 on Amazon, Top 5 on iTunes, number 2 on Barnes and Noble and Top 5 on KOBO. She has sold over two and a half million copies worldwide.

In her spare time, she doesn't tend to get much, she enjoys spending time walking her dog in rural Herefordshire, UK.

Her love of reading and specifically the devious minds of killers is what led her to pen her first book in the genre she adores.

Look out for more books coming in the future in the cozy mystery genre.

Facebook.com/Mel-Comley-264745836884860
Twitter.com/Melcom1
Bookbub.com/authors/m-a-comley

Made in the USA
Middletown, DE
26 May 2020